Thumbelina

STONE ARCH BOOKS
MINNEAPOLIS   SAN DIEGO

Graphic Spin is published by Stone Arch Books
151 Good Counsel Drive, P.O. Box 669
Mankato, Minnesota 56002
www.stonearchbooks.com

Library of Congress Cataloging-in-Publication Data

Powell, Martin.
 Thumbelina : the graphic novel / by Hans Christian Andersen ; retold by Martin Powell ;
illustrated by Sarah Horne.
    p. cm. -- (Graphic spin)
 ISBN 978-1-4342-1592-5 (lib. bdg.) -- ISBN 978-1-4342-1741-7 (pbk.)
 1. Graphic novels. [1. Graphic novels. 2. Fairy tales.] I. Horne, Sarah, 1979- ill. II. Andersen,
H. C. (Hans Christian), 1805-1875. Tommelise. III. Title.
 PZ7.7.P69Th 2010
 741.5'973--dc22
                                    2009010531

Summary: After seeking the help of a strange old woman, Gerta is amazed to see a tiny girl emerge
from the blooming petals of a magical flower! Gerta has always wanted a child of her own, so
she adopts the tiny maiden and names her Thumbelina. While Gerta sleeps, a strange creature
creeps forth from the darkness and steals Thumbelina into the night. Lost and alone in a forest,
Thumbelina must seek the aid of the forest creatures if she is to ever see Gerta again.

Creative Director: Heather Kindseth
Graphic Designer: Hilary Wacholz
Cover Colorist: Gerardo Sandoval

J
GRAPHIC
NOVEL

Printed in the United States of America

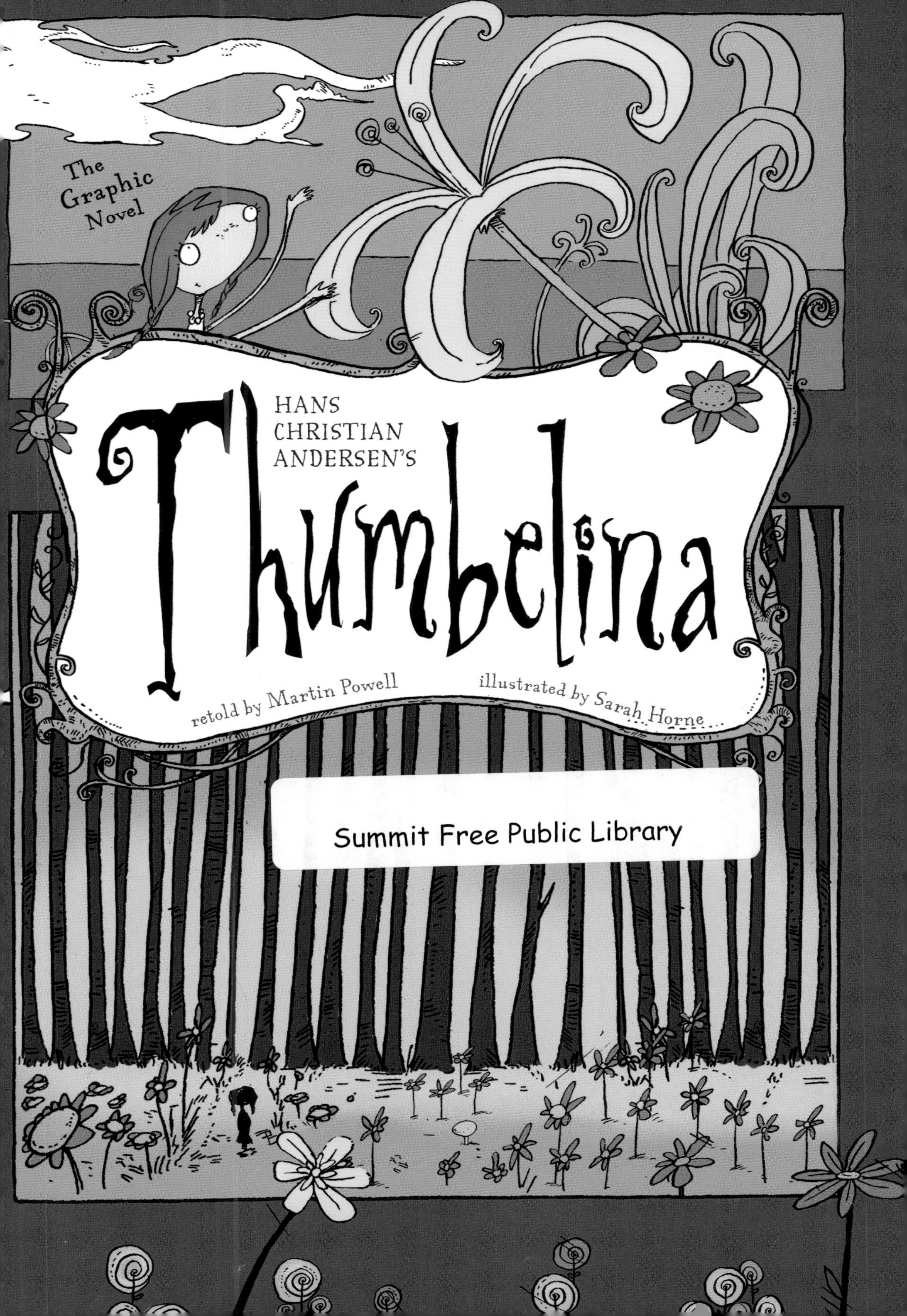
The Graphic Novel
HANS CHRISTIAN ANDERSEN'S
Thumbelina
retold by Martin Powell
illustrated by Sarah Horne
Summit Free Public Library

CAST OF CHARACTERS

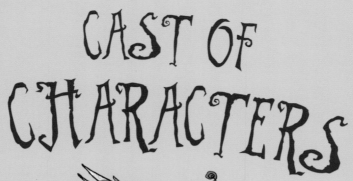

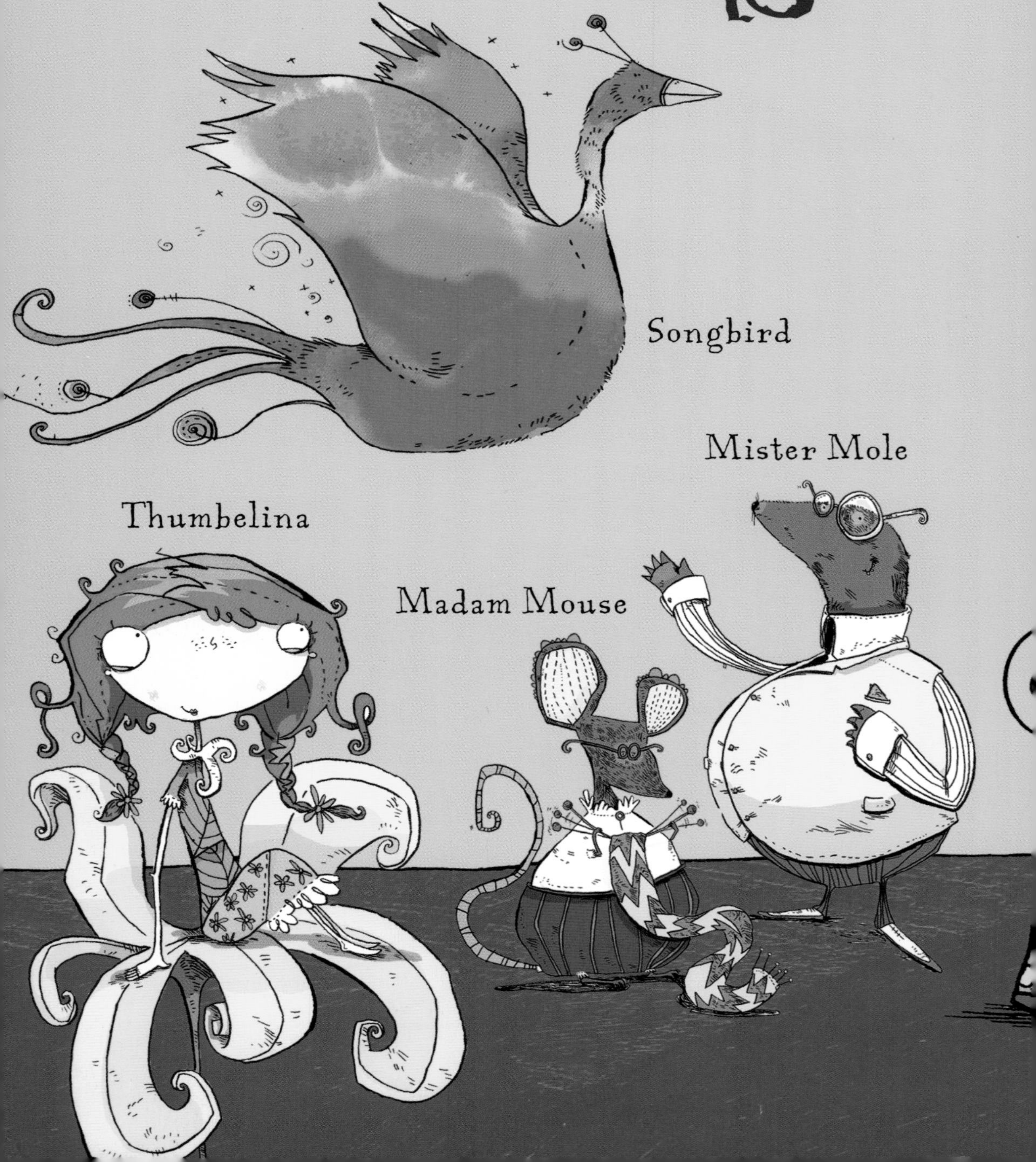
Songbird
Mister Mole
Thumbelina
Madam Mouse

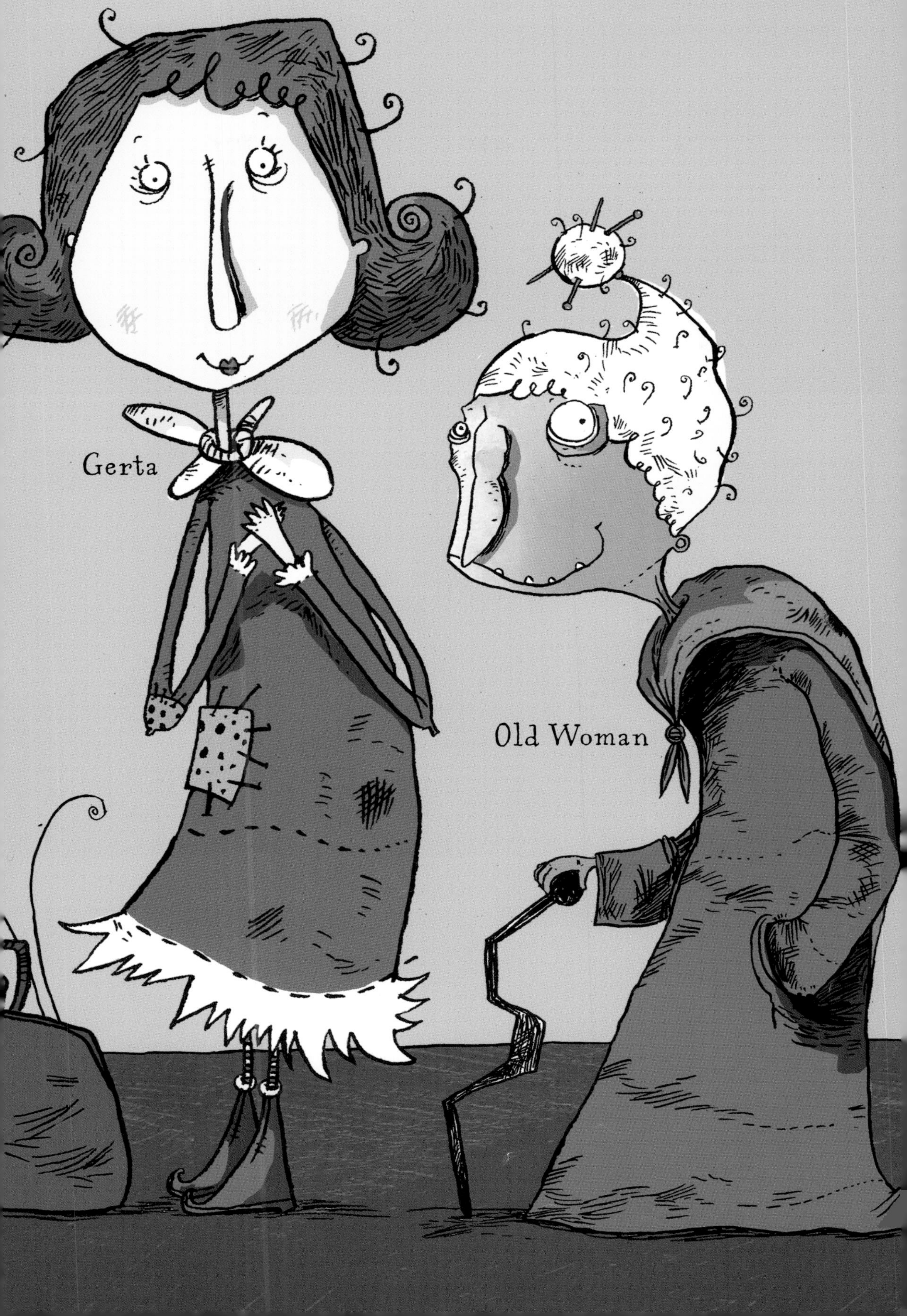
Gerta
Old Woman

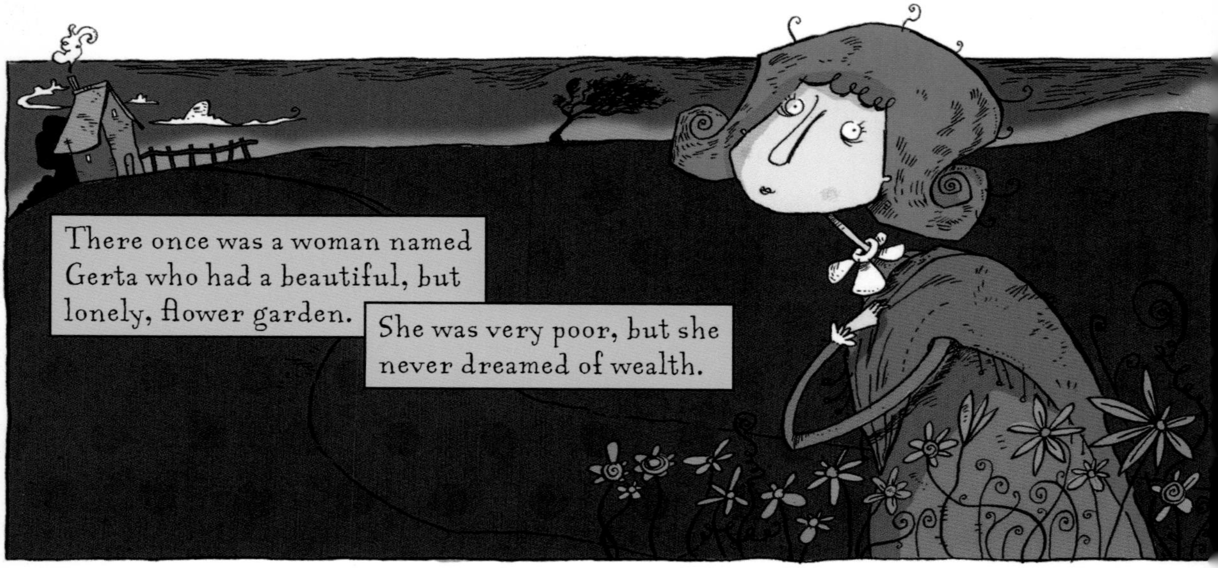
There once was a woman named Gerta who had a beautiful, but lonely, flower garden.
She was very poor, but she never dreamed of wealth.

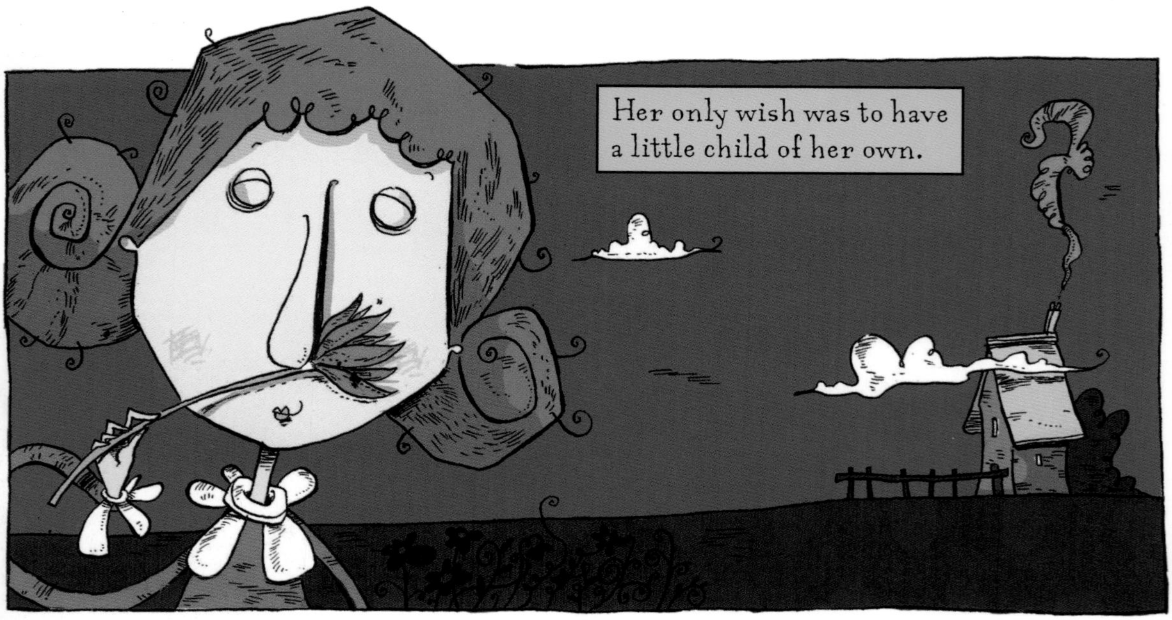
Her only wish was to have a little child of her own.

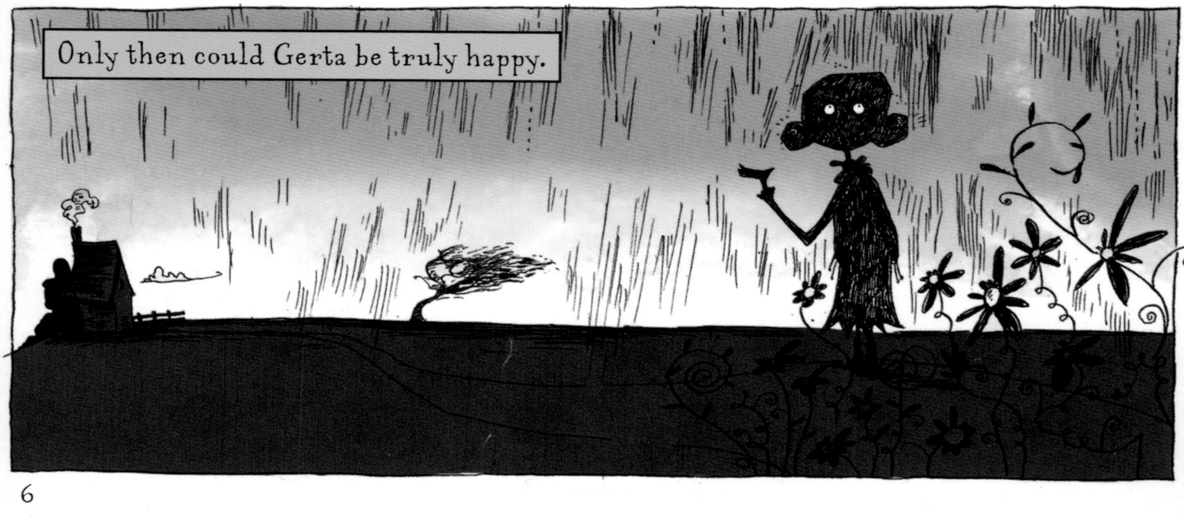
Only then could Gerta be truly happy.

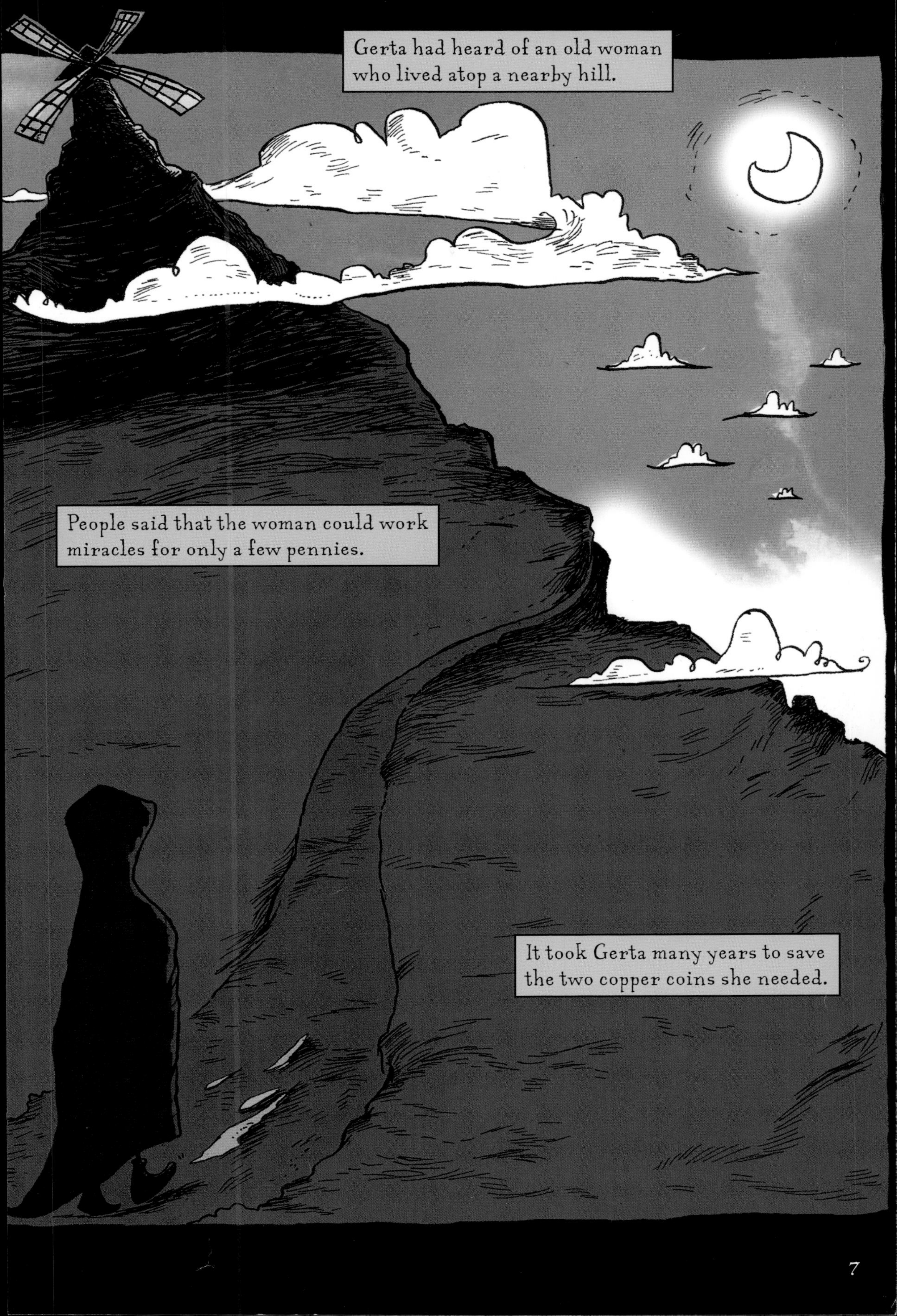
Gerta had heard of an old woman who lived atop a nearby hill.
People said that the woman could work miracles for only a few pennies.
It took Gerta many years to save the two copper coins she needed.

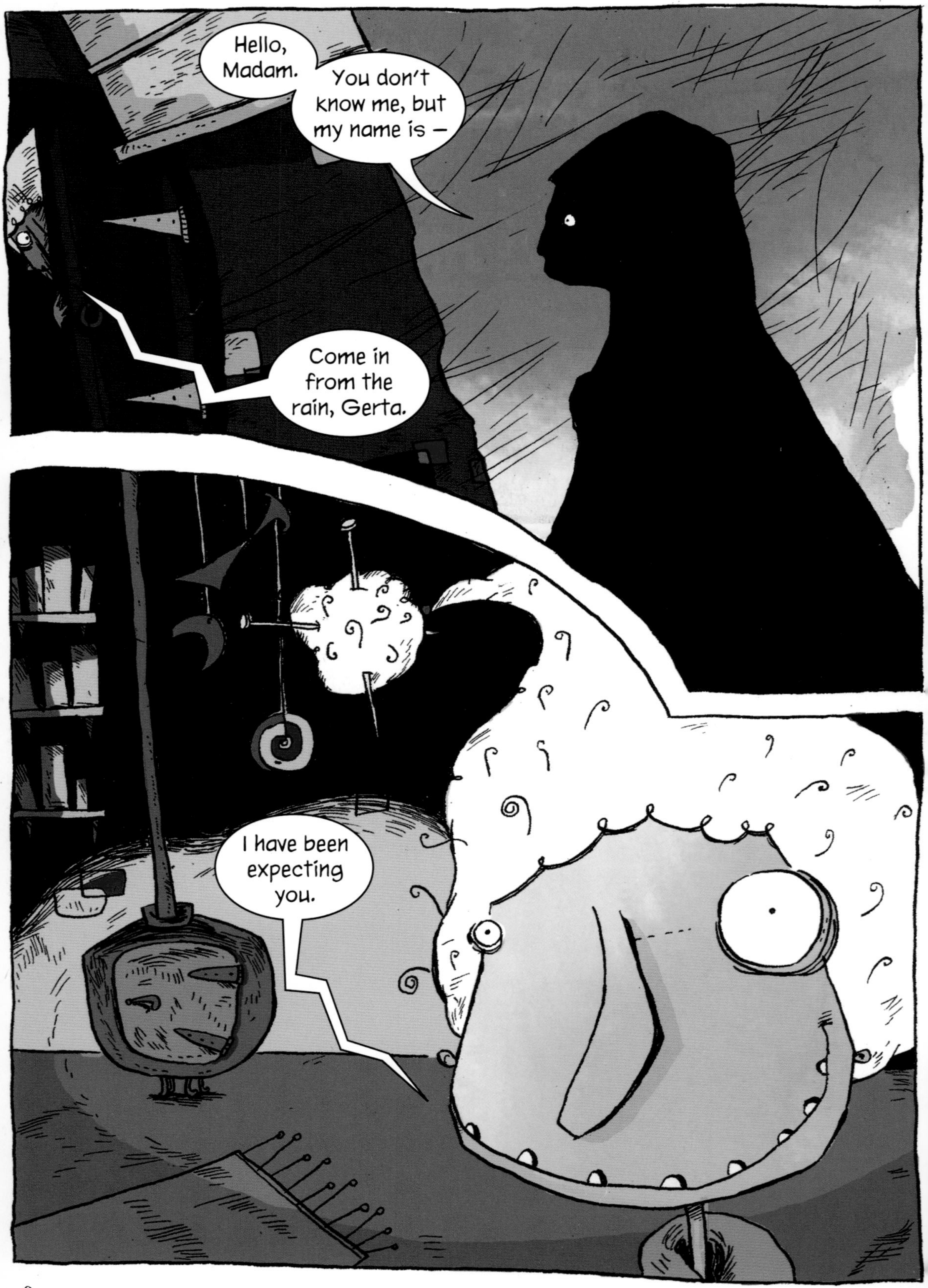
Hello, Madam.
You don't know me, but my name is —
Come in from the rain, Gerta.
I have been expecting you.

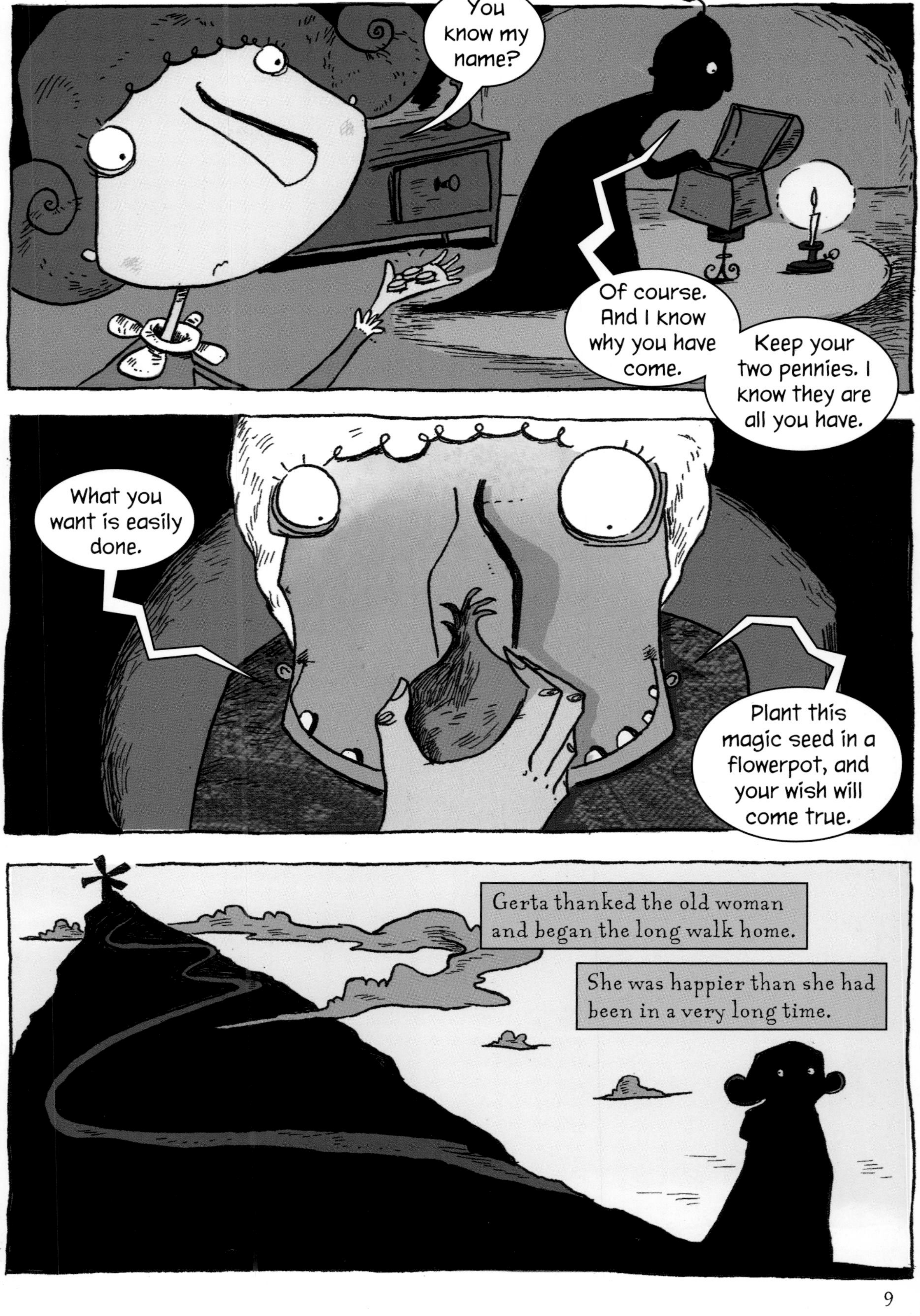
You know my name?
Of course. And I know why you have come.
Keep your two pennies. I know they are all you have.
What you want is easily done.
Plant this magic seed in a flowerpot, and your wish will come true.
Gerta thanked the old woman and began the long walk home.
She was happier than she had been in a very long time.

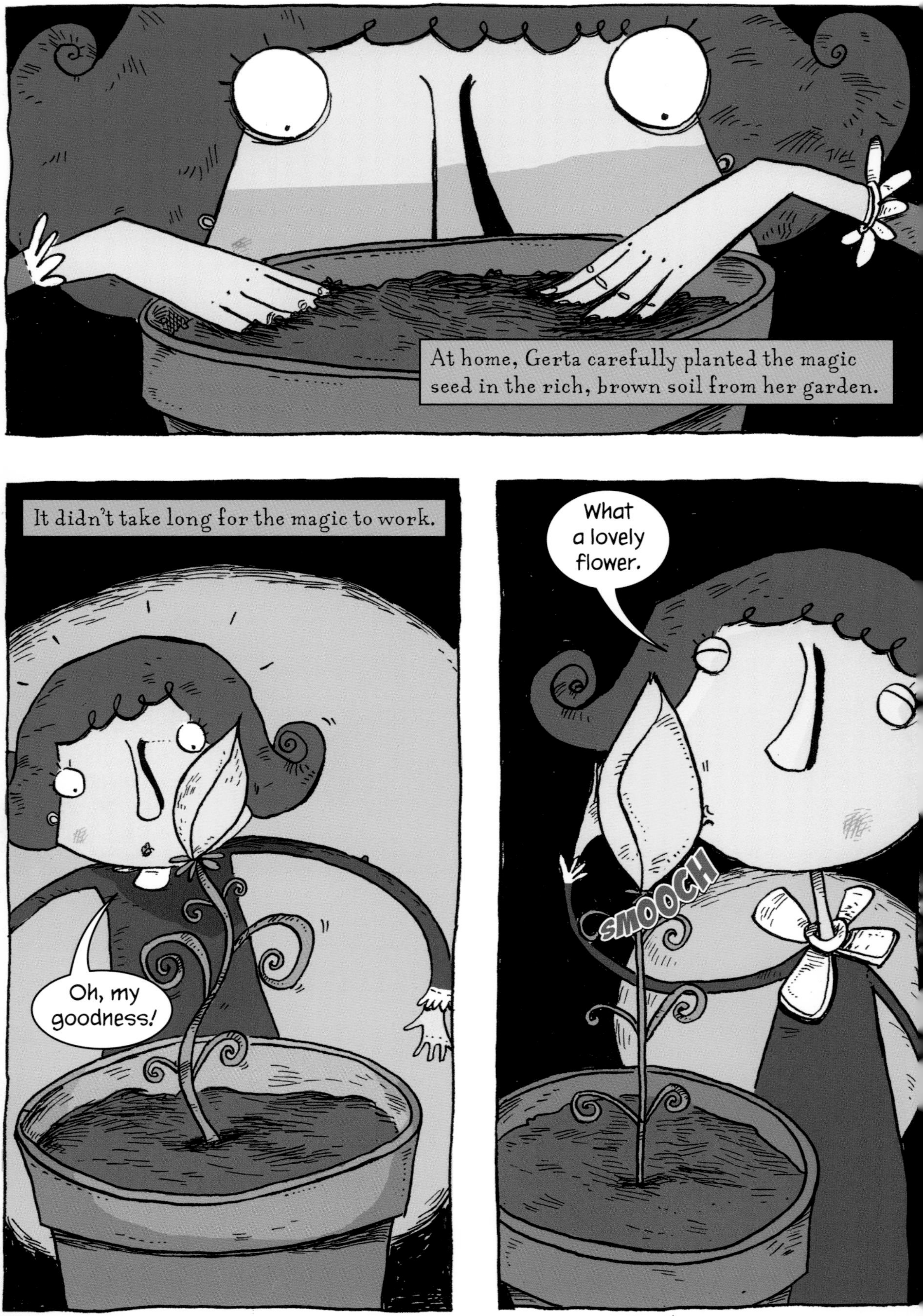
At home, Gerta carefully planted the magic seed in the rich, brown soil from her garden.
It didn't take long for the magic to work.
Oh, my goodness!
What a lovely flower.
SMOOCH

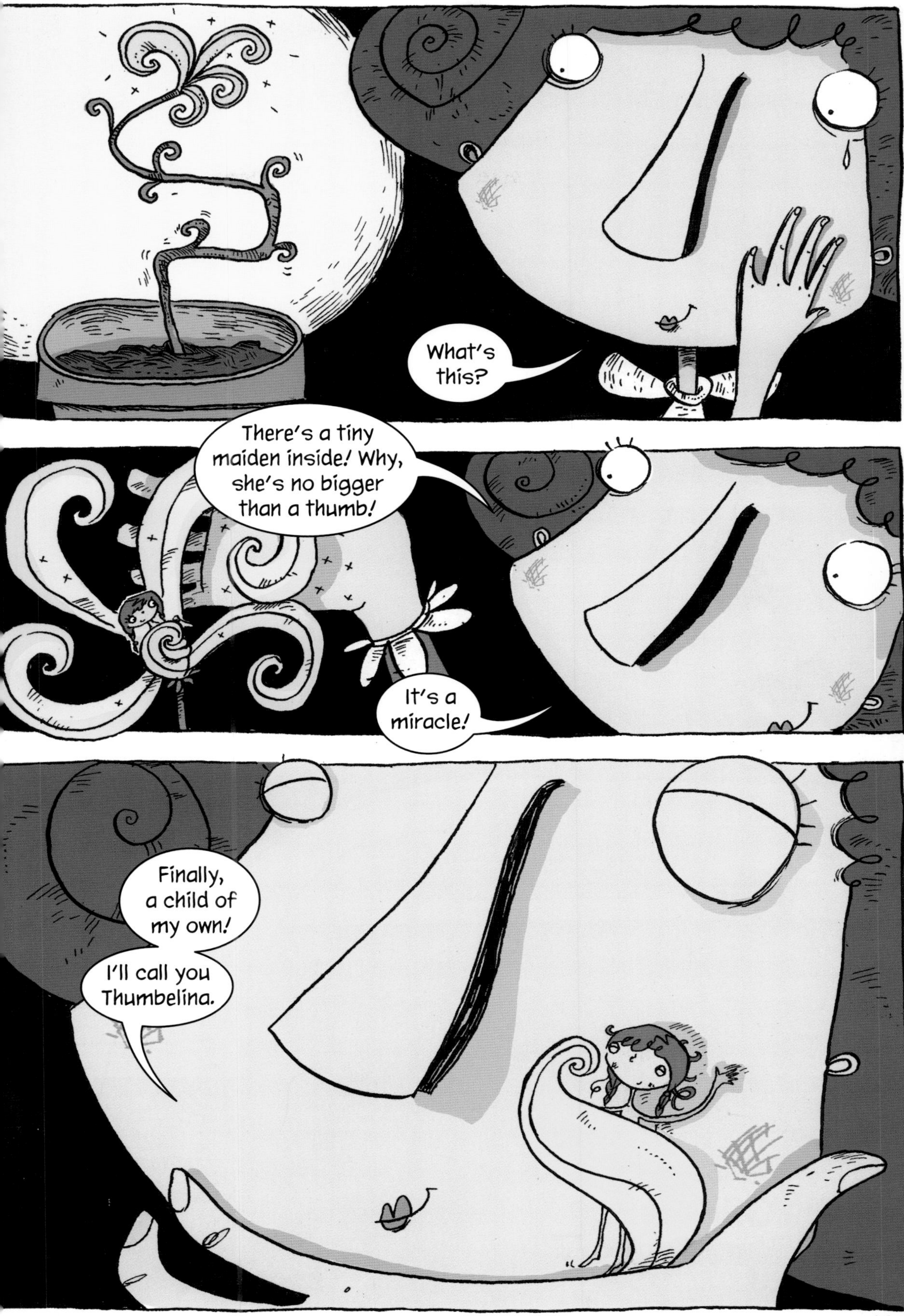

What's this?
There's a tiny maiden inside! Why, she's no bigger than a thumb!
It's a miracle!
Finally, a child of my own!
I'll call you Thumbelina.

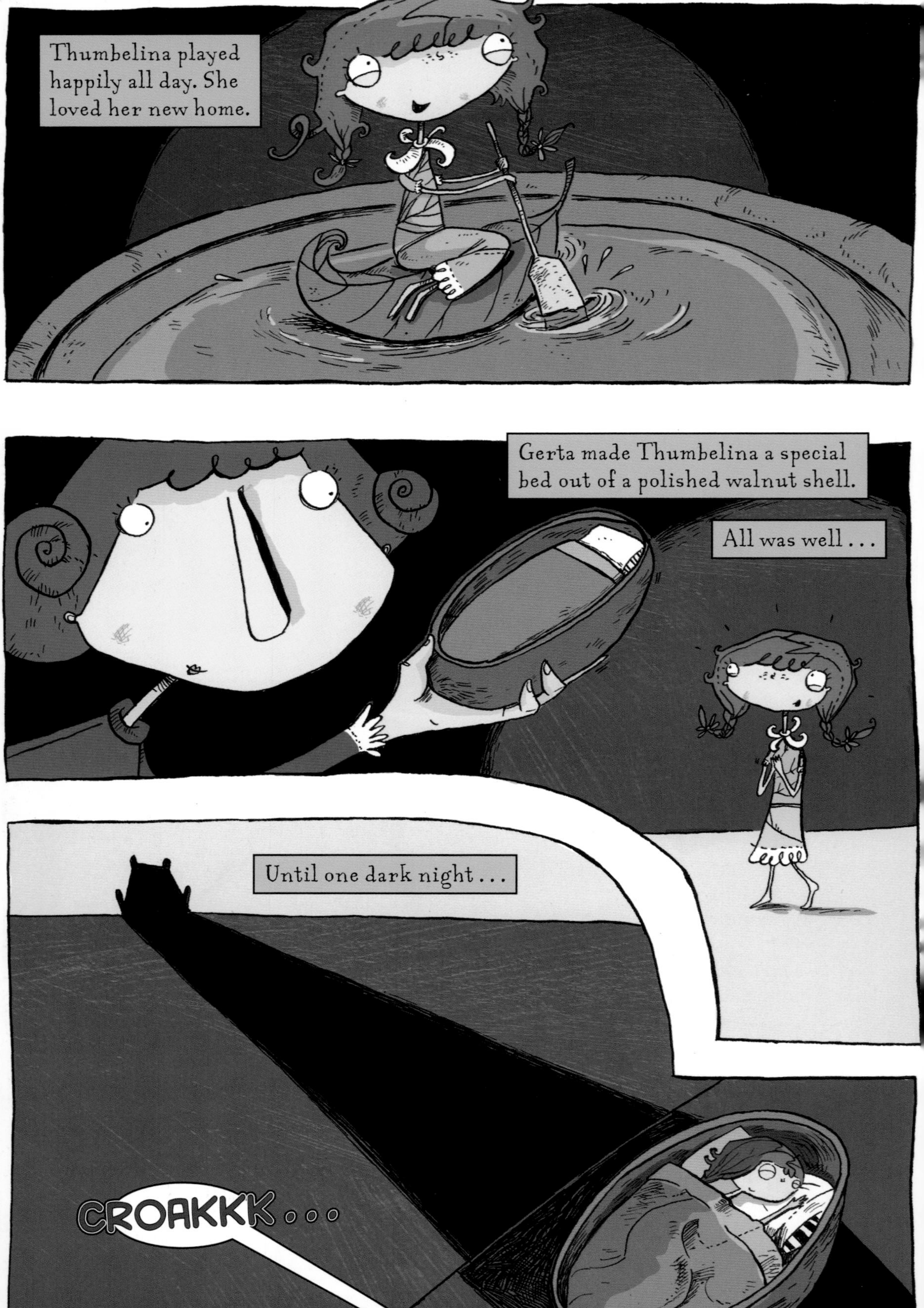
Thumbelina played happily all day. She loved her new home.
Gerta made Thumbelina a special bed out of a polished walnut shell.
All was well . . .
Until one dark night . . .
CROAKK . . .

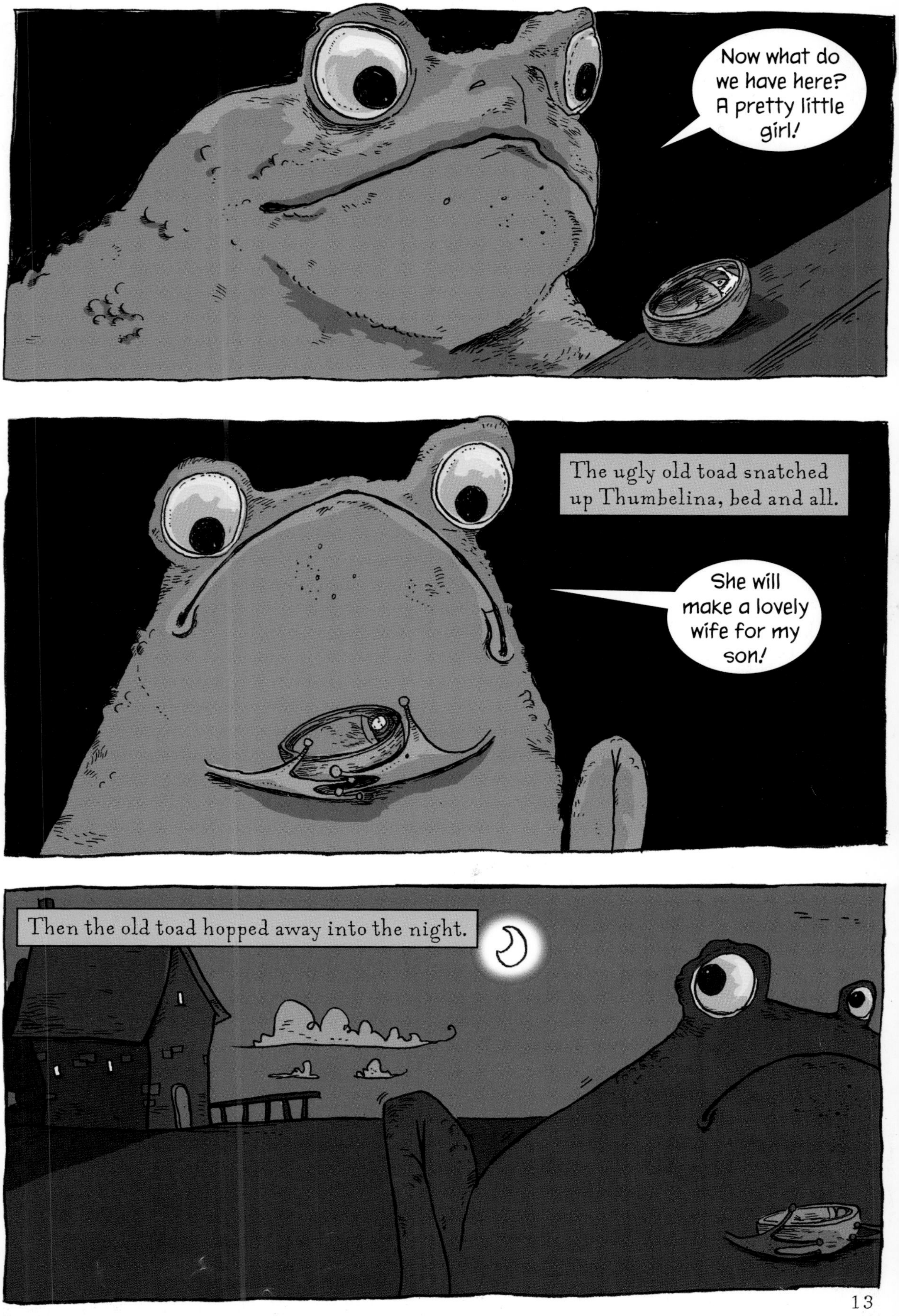

Now what do we have here? A pretty little girl!
The ugly old toad snatched up Thumbelina, bed and all.
She will make a lovely wife for my son!
Then the old toad hopped away into the night.

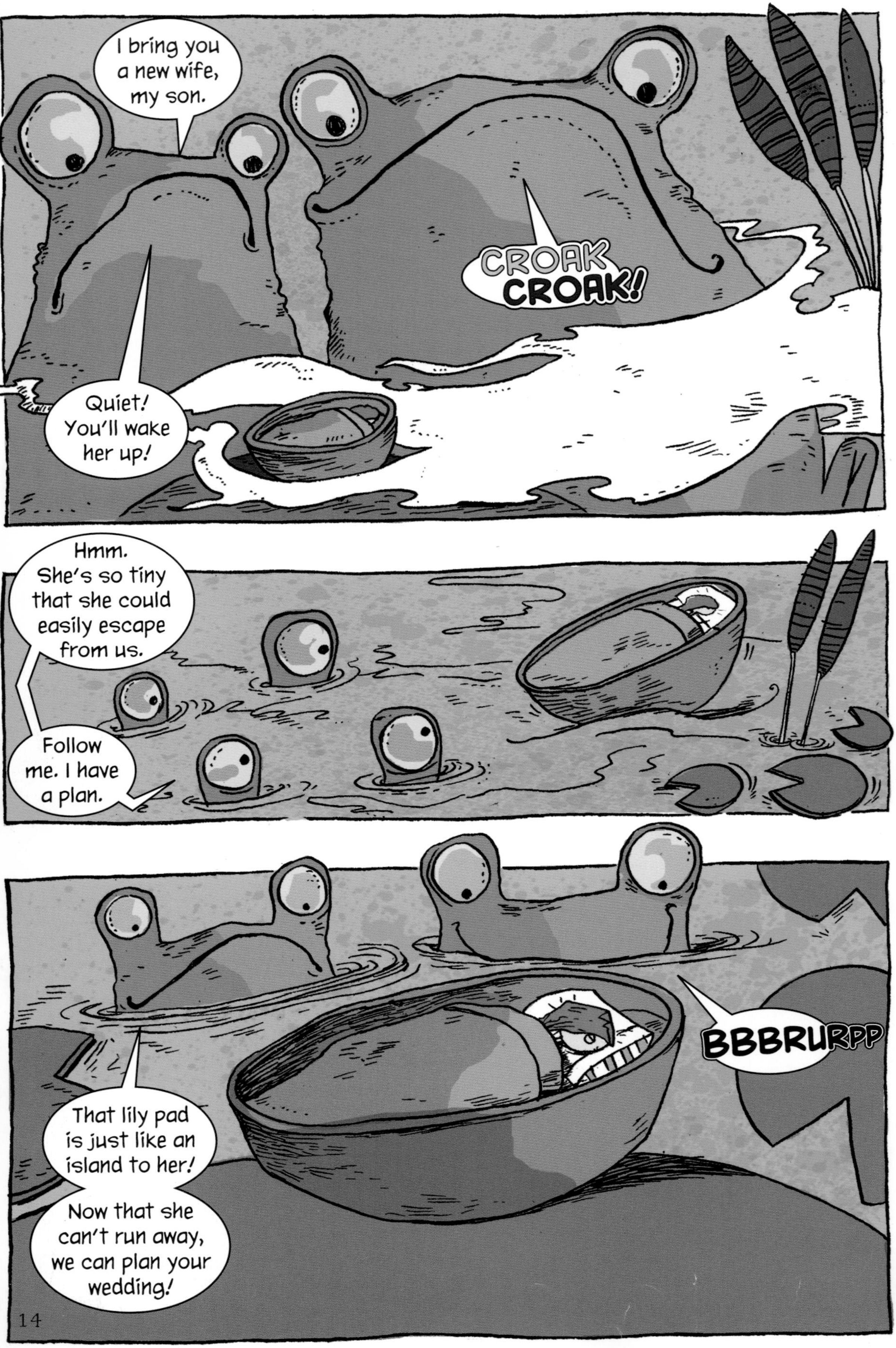
I bring you a new wife, my son.
CROAK CROAK!
Quiet! You'll wake her up!
Hmm. She's so tiny that she could easily escape from us.
Follow me. I have a plan.
BBBRURPP
That lily pad is just like an island to her!
Now that she can't run away, we can plan your wedding!

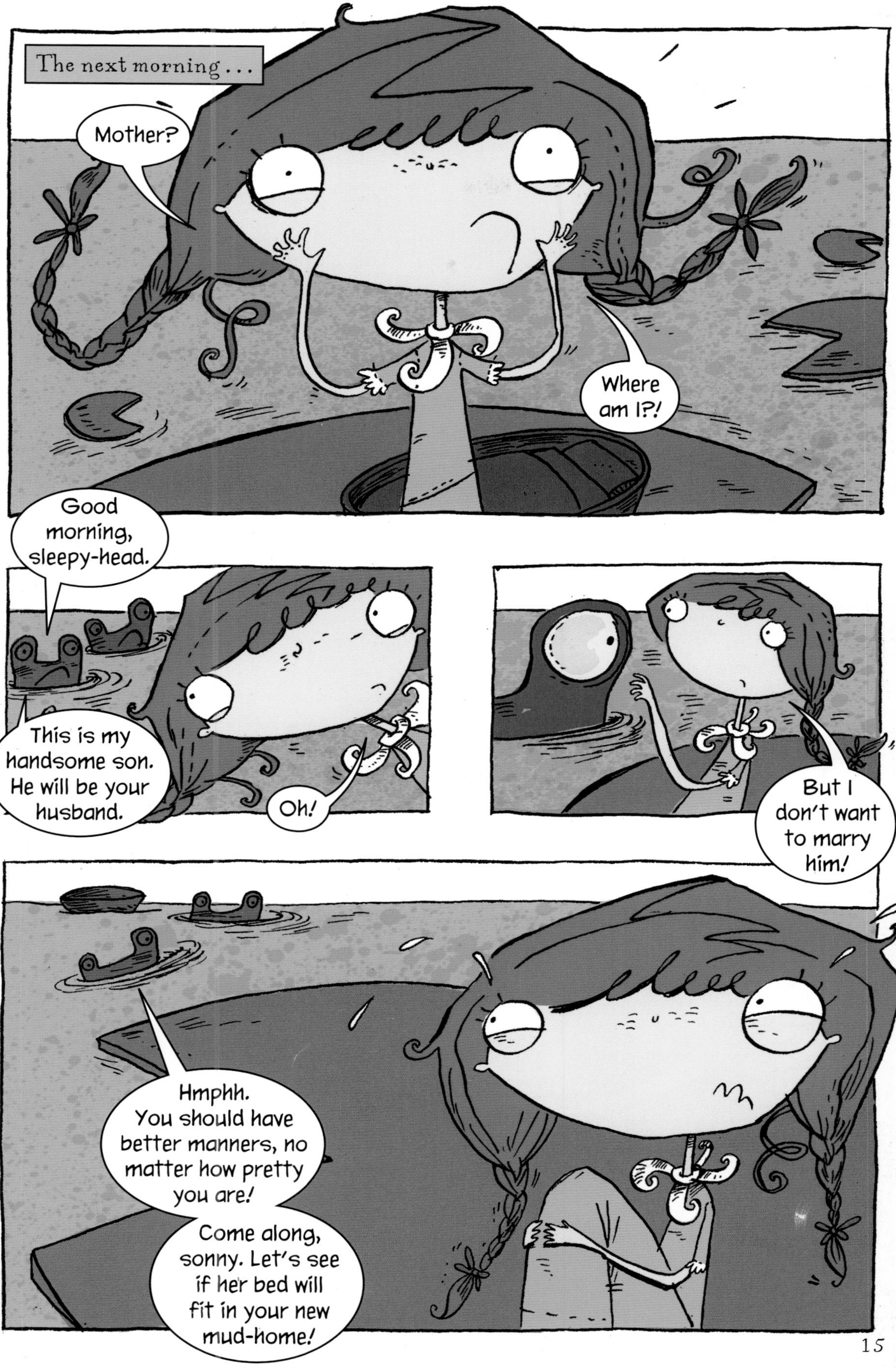
The next morning . . .
Mother?
Where am I?!
Good morning, sleepy-head.
This is my handsome son. He will be your husband.
Oh!
But I don't want to marry him!
Hmphh. You should have better manners, no matter how pretty you are!
Come along, sonny. Let's see if her bed will fit in your new mud-home!

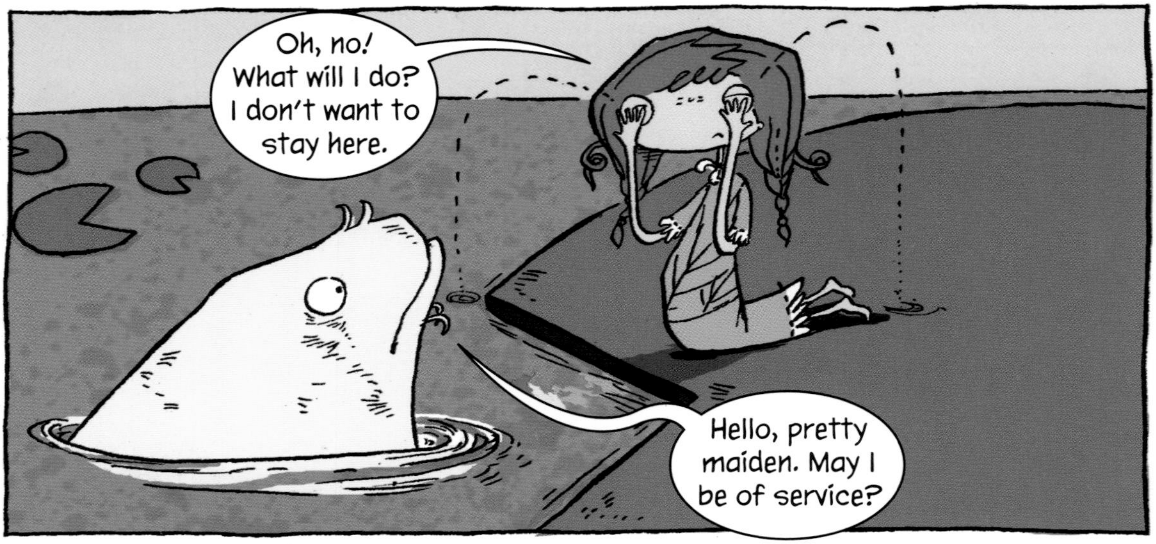
Oh, no! What will I do? I don't want to stay here.
Hello, pretty maiden. May I be of service?

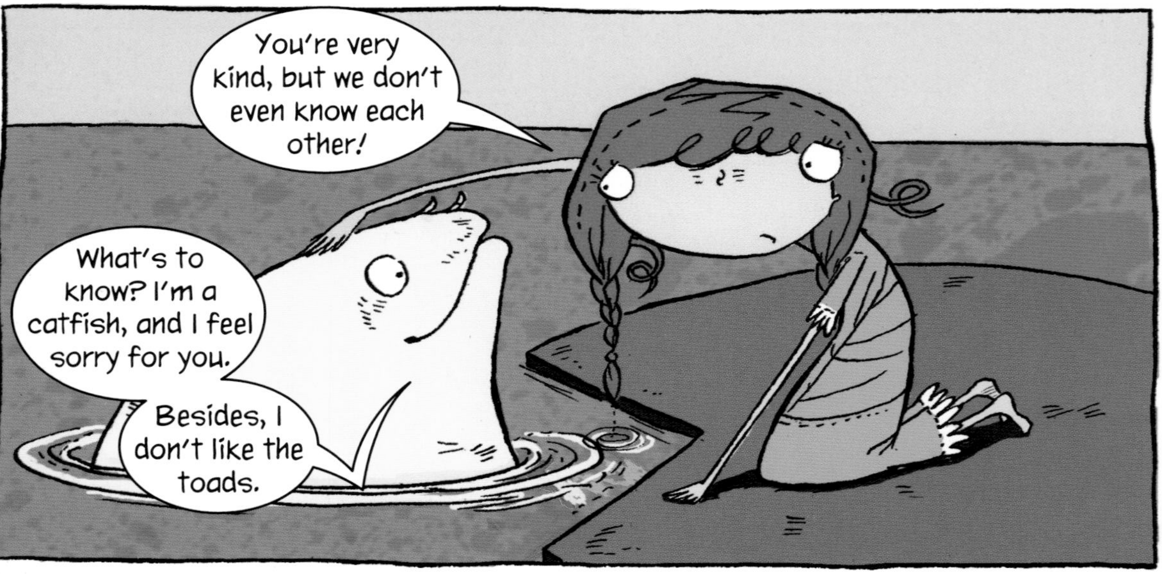
You're very kind, but we don't even know each other!
What's to know? I'm a catfish, and I feel sorry for you.
Besides, I don't like the toads.

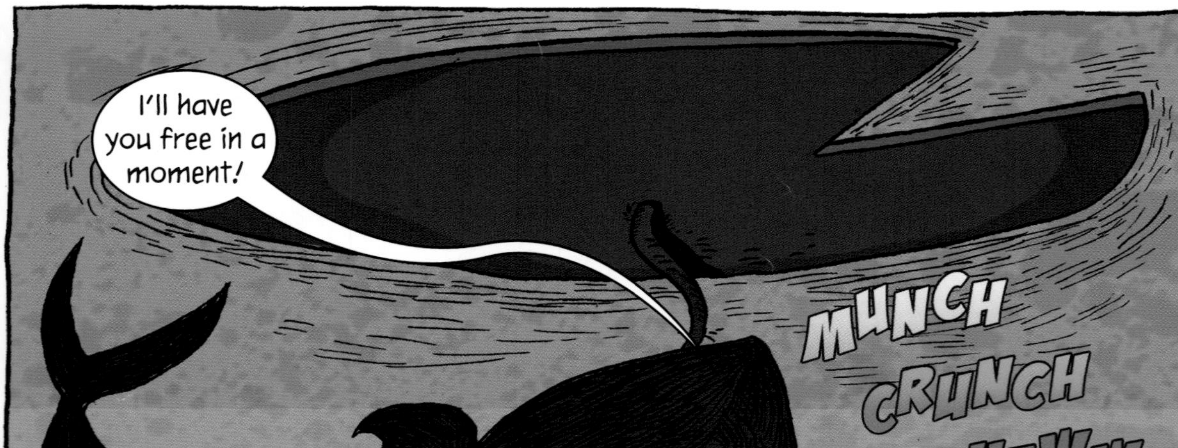
I'll have you free in a moment!
MUNCH
CRUNCH
CHEWW

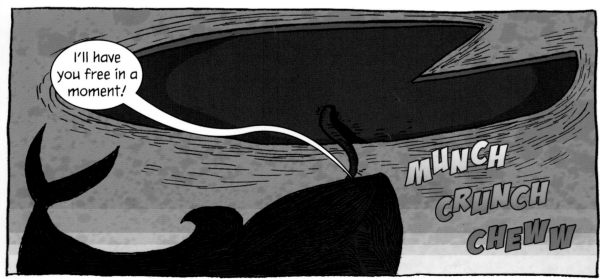

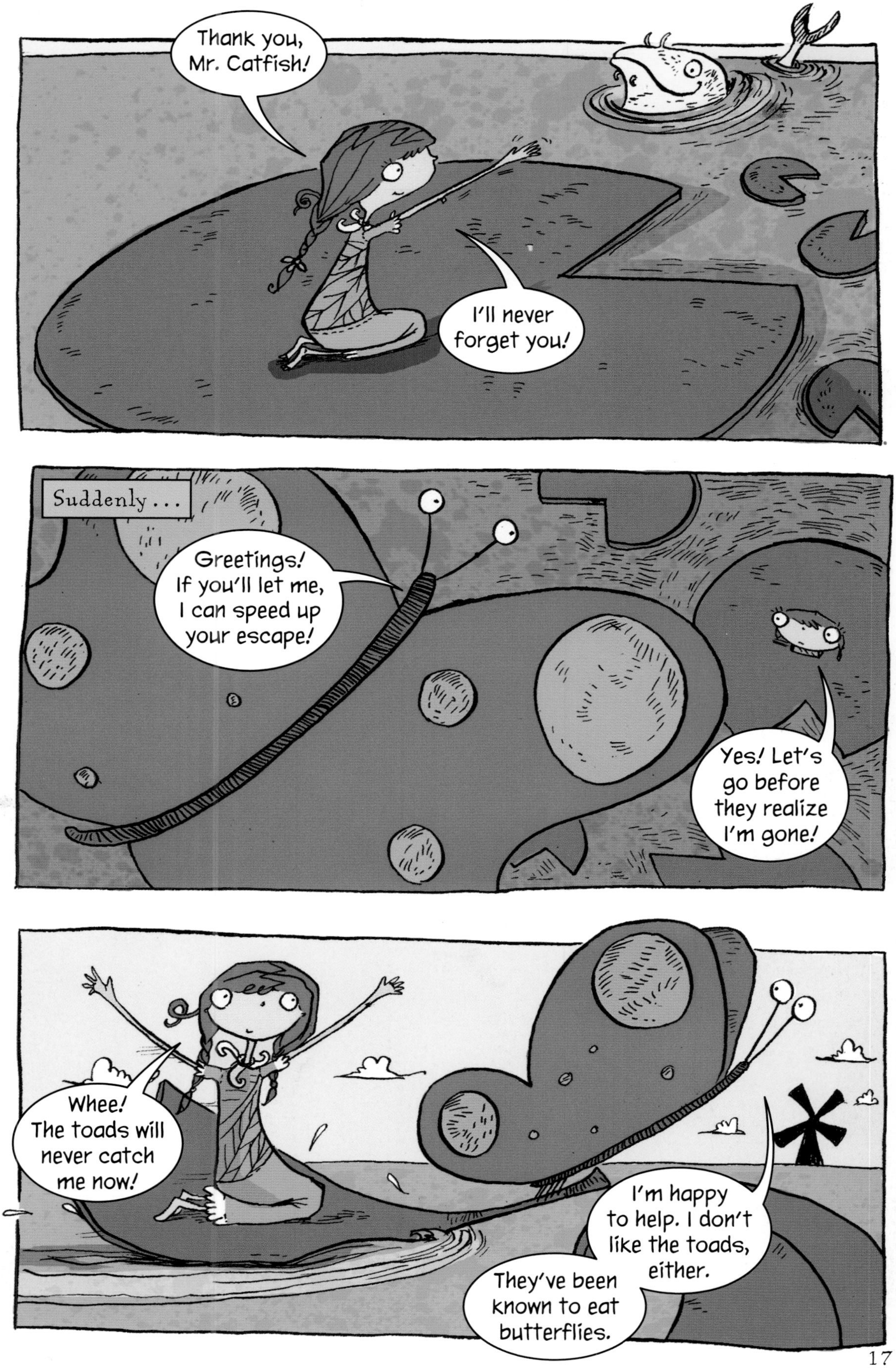
Thank you, Mr. Catfish!
I'll never forget you!
Suddenly . . .
Greetings! If you'll let me, I can speed up your escape!
Yes! Let's go before they realize I'm gone!
Whee! The toads will never catch me now!
I'm happy to help. I don't like the toads, either.
They've been known to eat butterflies.

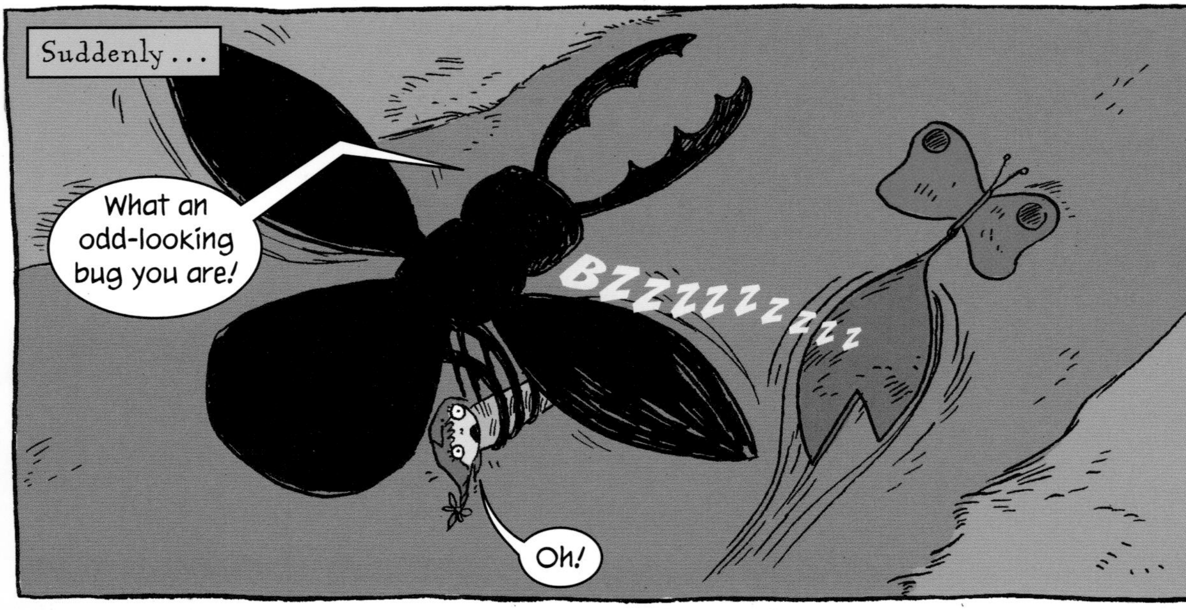
Suddenly . . .
What an odd-looking bug you are!
BZZZZZZZZZ
Oh!

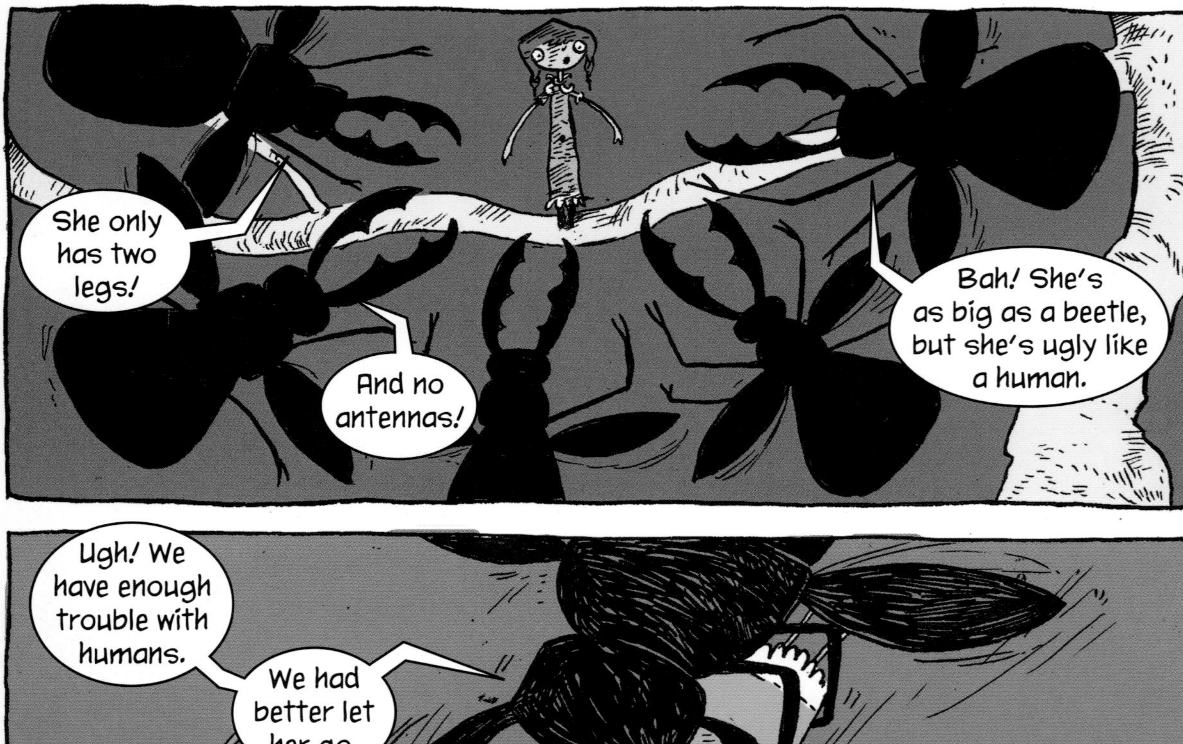
She only has two legs!
And no antennas!
Bah! She's as big as a beetle, but she's ugly like a human.

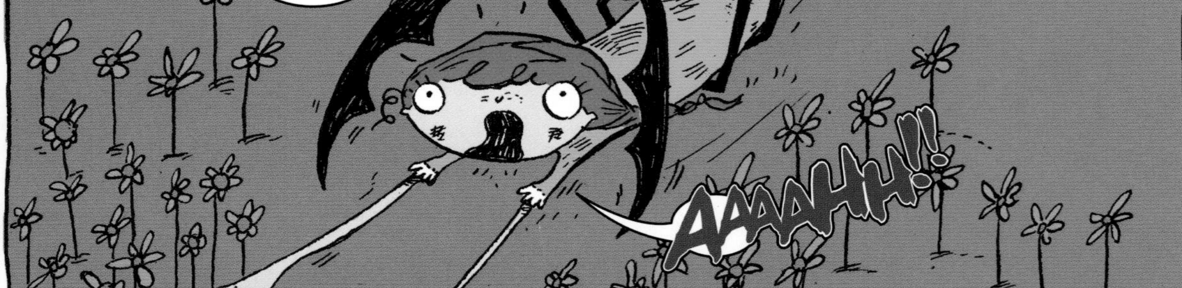
Ugh! We have enough trouble with humans.
We had better let her go.
AAAAHH!!

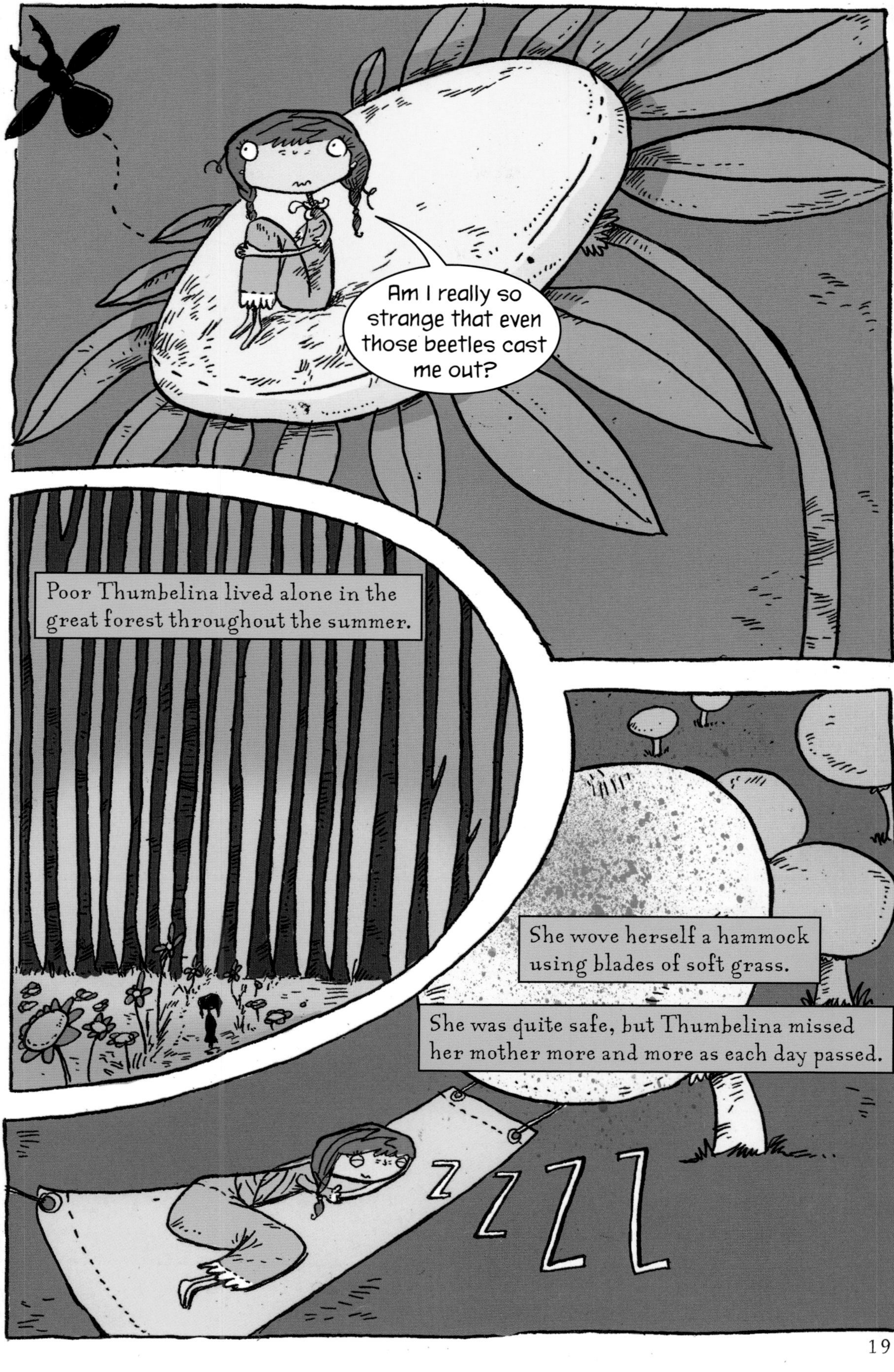
Am I really so strange that even those beetles cast me out?
Poor Thumbelina lived alone in the great forest throughout the summer.
She wove herself a hammock using blades of soft grass.
She was quite safe, but Thumbelina missed her mother more and more as each day passed.
ZZZ

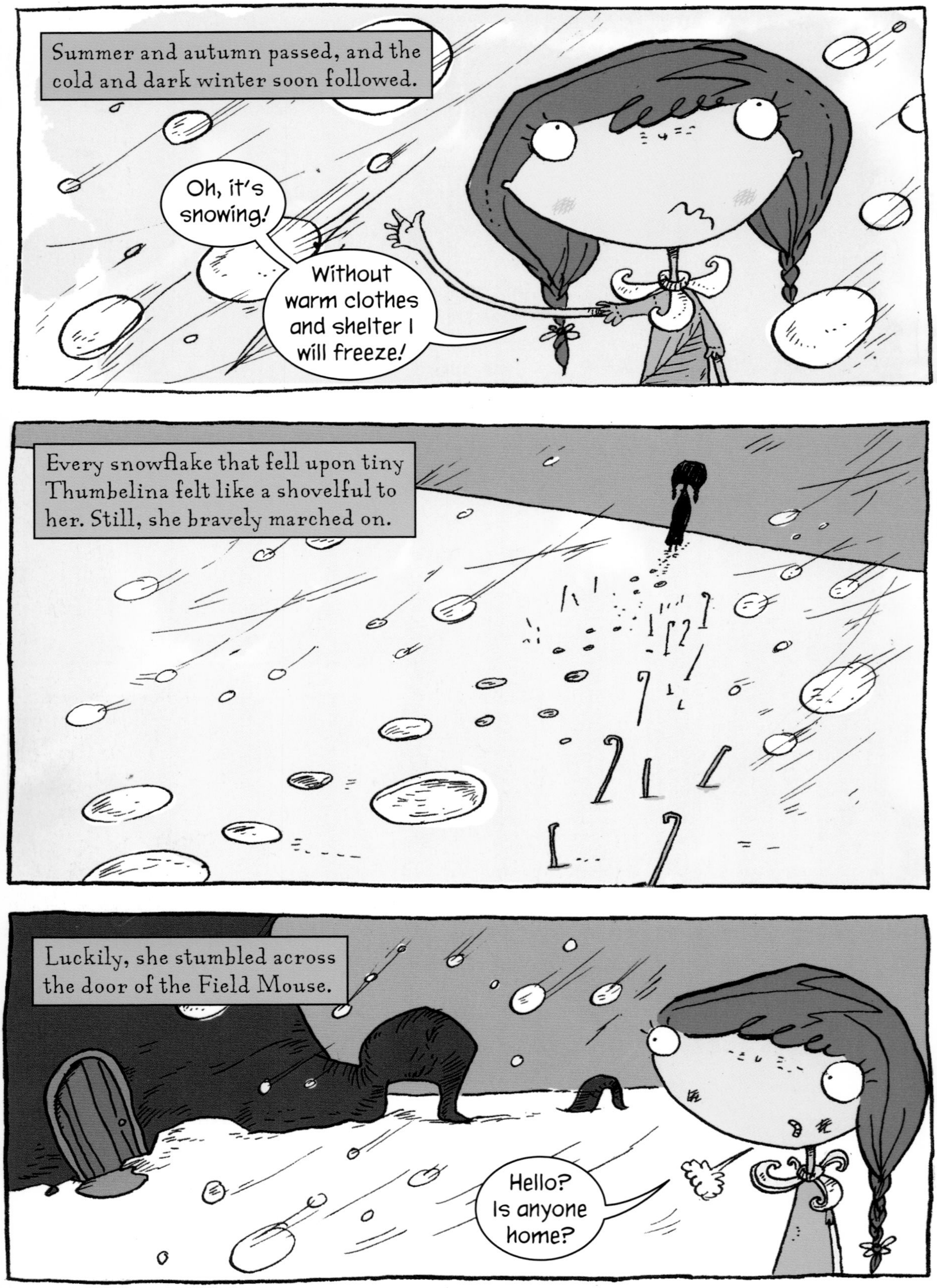
Summer and autumn passed, and the cold and dark winter soon followed.
Oh, it's snowing!
Without warm clothes and shelter I will freeze!
Every snowflake that fell upon tiny Thumbelina felt like a shovelful to her. Still, she bravely marched on.
Luckily, she stumbled across the door of the Field Mouse.
Hello? Is anyone home?

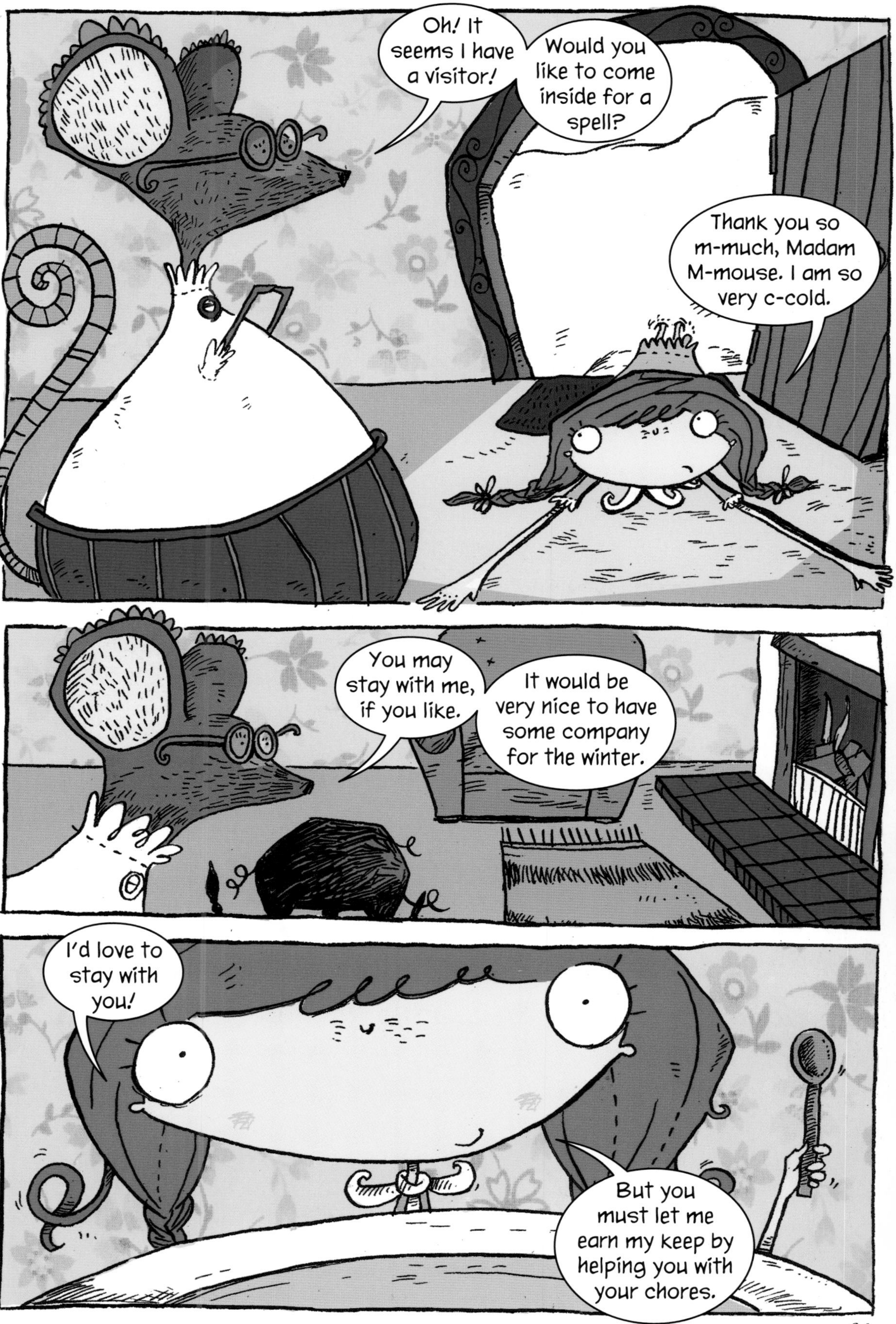
Oh! It seems I have a visitor!
Would you like to come inside for a spell?
Thank you so m-much, Madam M-mouse. I am so very c-cold.
You may stay with me, if you like.
It would be very nice to have some company for the winter.
I'd love to stay with you!
But you must let me earn my keep by helping you with your chores.

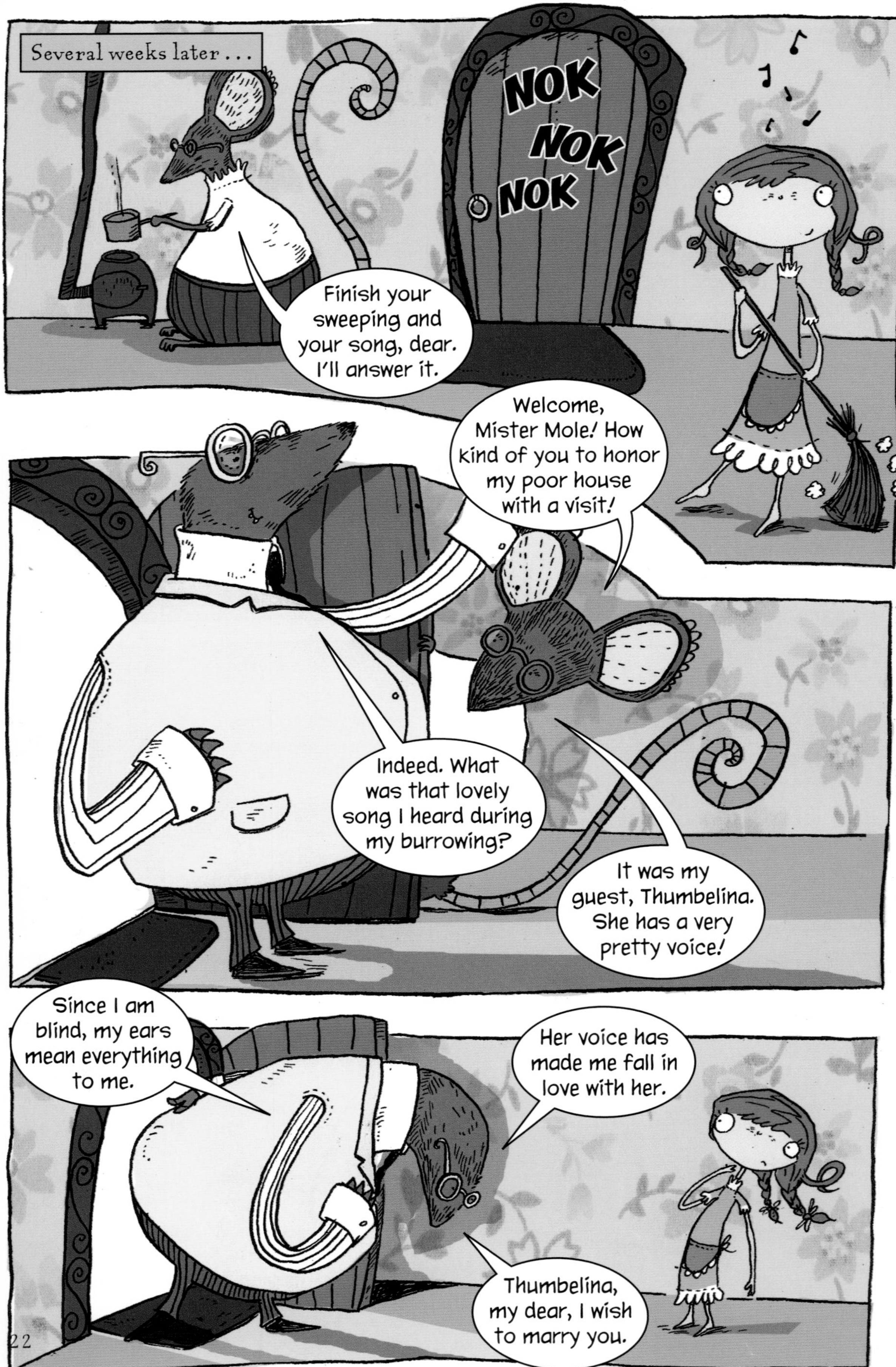

Several weeks later . . .
NOK NOK NOK
Finish your sweeping and your song, dear. I'll answer it.
Welcome, Mister Mole! How kind of you to honor my poor house with a visit!
Indeed. What was that lovely song I heard during my burrowing?
It was my guest, Thumbelina. She has a very pretty voice!
Since I am blind, my ears mean everything to me.
Her voice has made me fall in love with her.
Thumbelina, my dear, I wish to marry you.

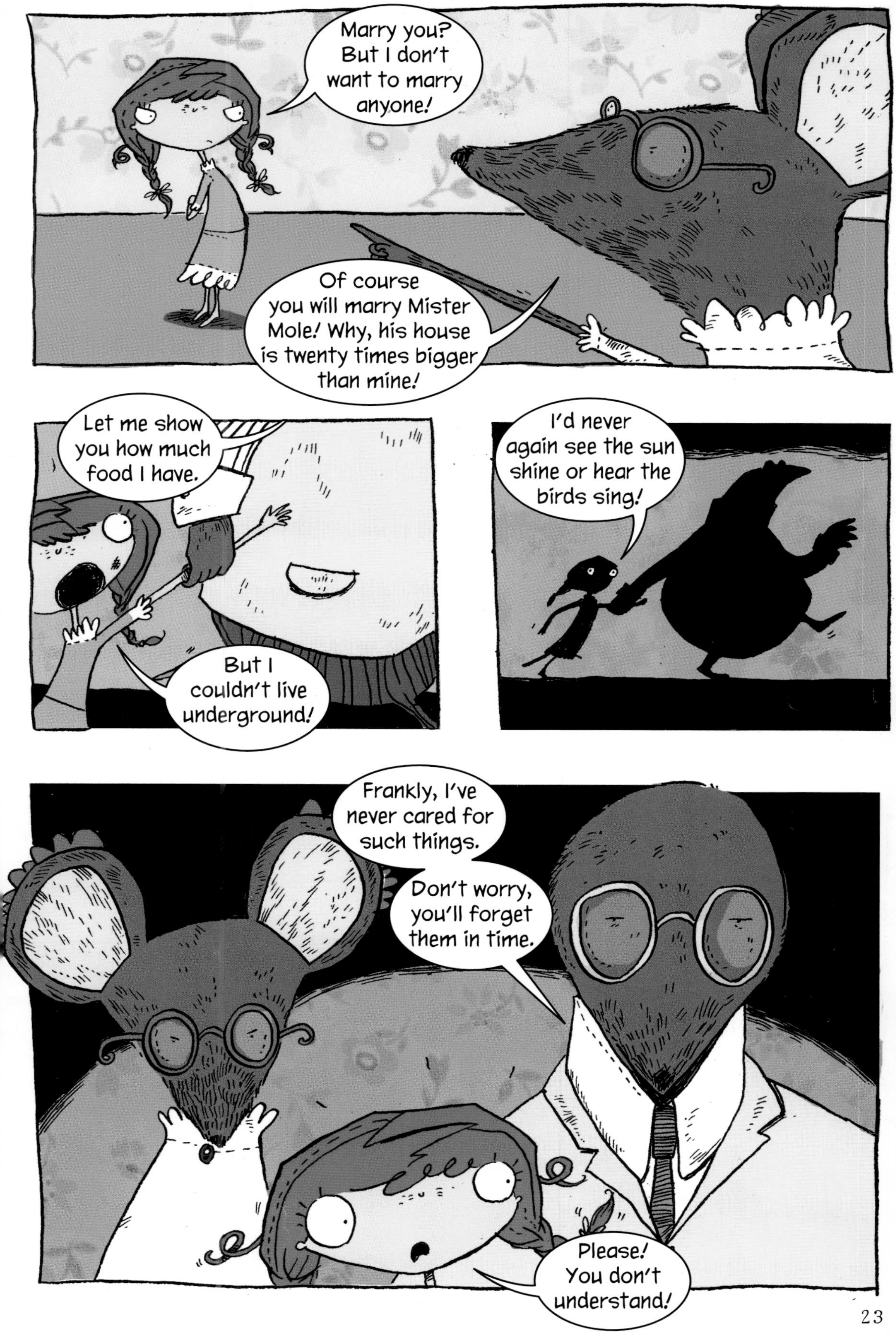
Marry you? But I don't want to marry anyone!
Of course you will marry Mister Mole! Why, his house is twenty times bigger than mine!
Let me show you how much food I have.
But I couldn't live underground!
I'd never again see the sun shine or hear the birds sing!
Frankly, I've never cared for such things.
Don't worry, you'll forget them in time.
Please! You don't understand!

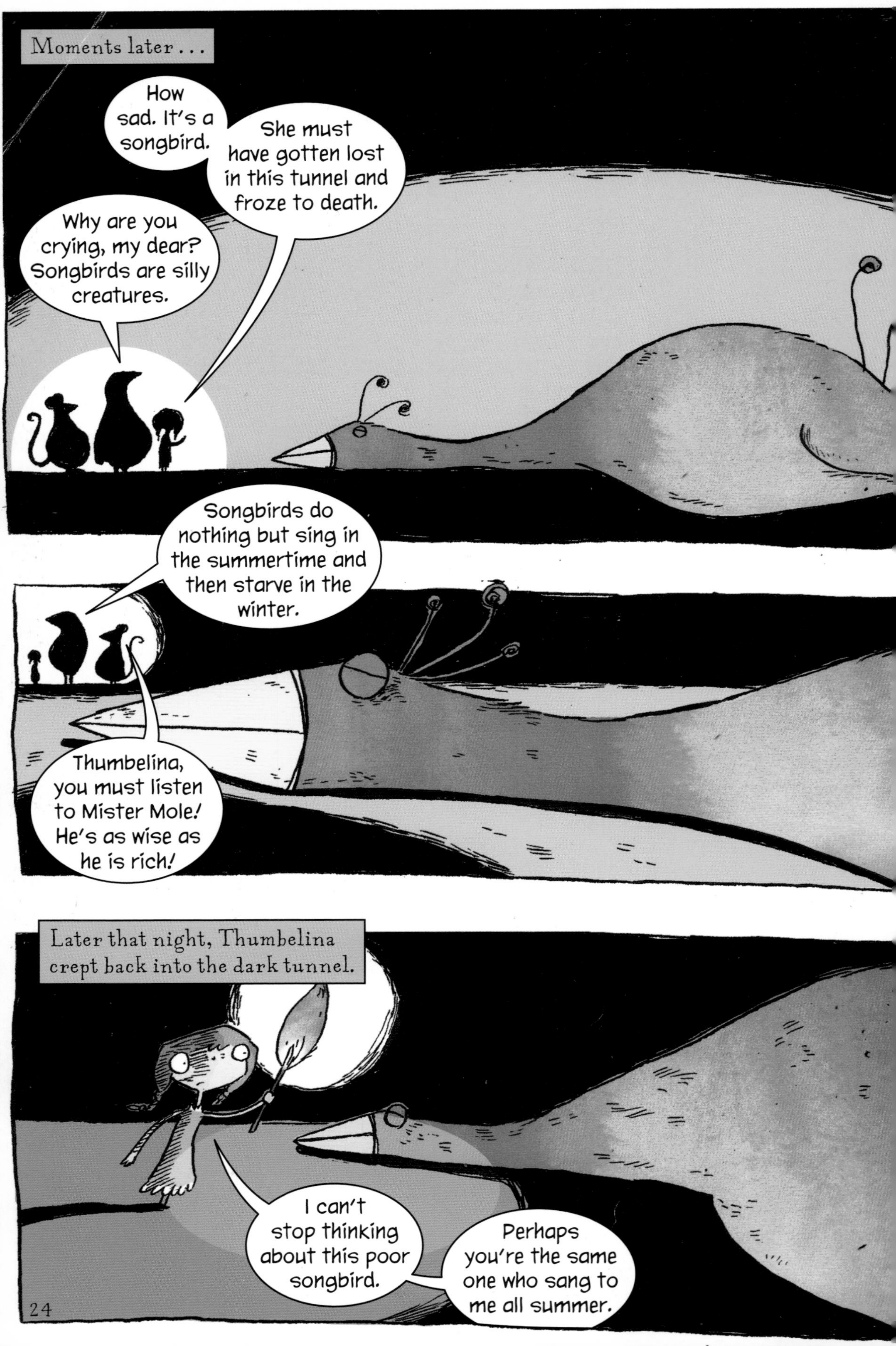
Moments later . . .
How sad. It's a songbird.
She must have gotten lost in this tunnel and froze to death.
Why are you crying, my dear? Songbirds are silly creatures.
Songbirds do nothing but sing in the summertime and then starve in the winter.
Thumbelina, you must listen to Mister Mole! He's as wise as he is rich!
Later that night, Thumbelina crept back into the dark tunnel.
I can't stop thinking about this poor songbird.
Perhaps you're the same one who sang to me all summer.

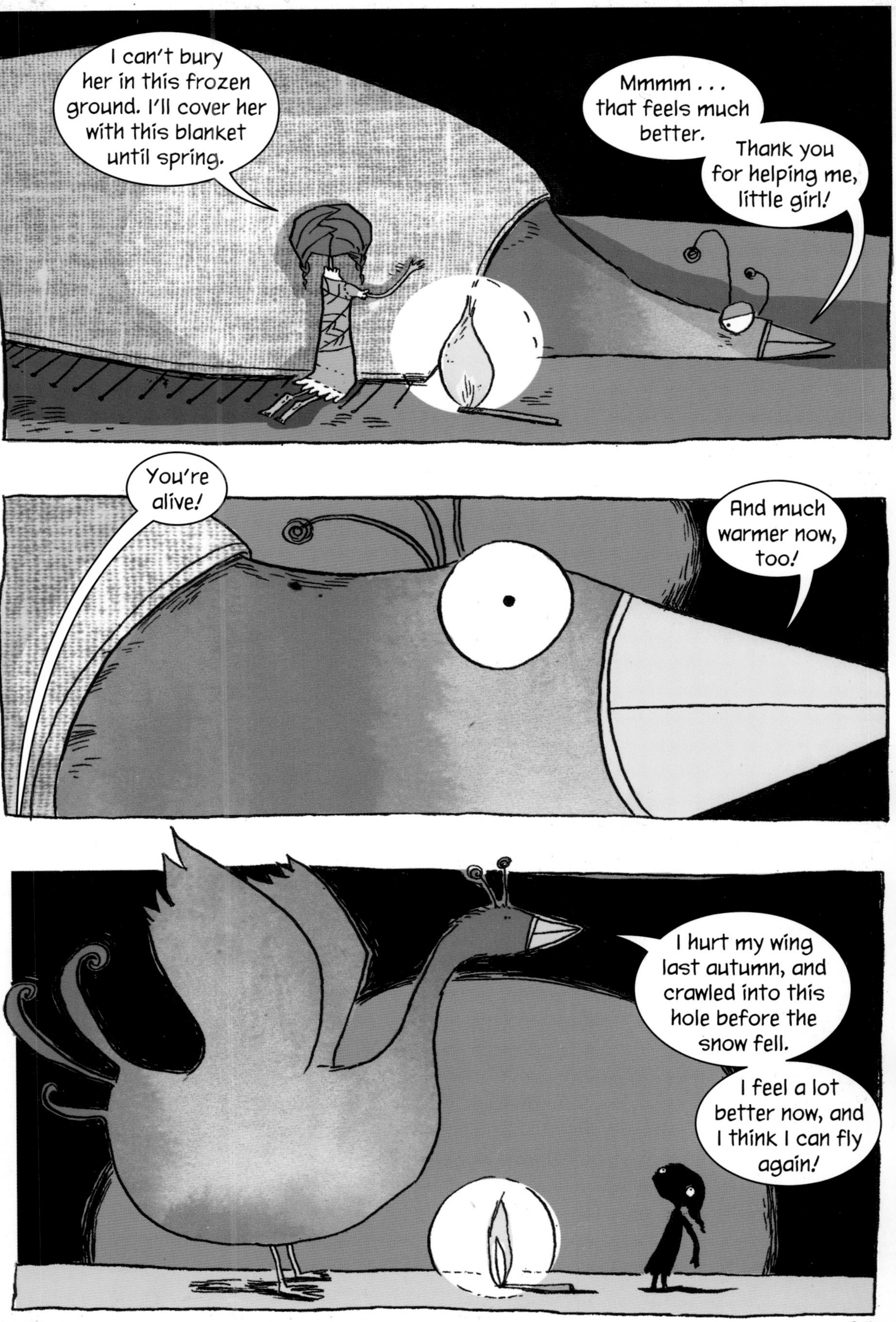
I can't bury her in this frozen ground. I'll cover her with this blanket until spring.
Mmmm . . . that feels much better.
Thank you for helping me, little girl!
You're alive!
And much warmer now, too!
I hurt my wing last autumn, and crawled into this hole before the snow fell.
I feel a lot better now, and I think I can fly again!

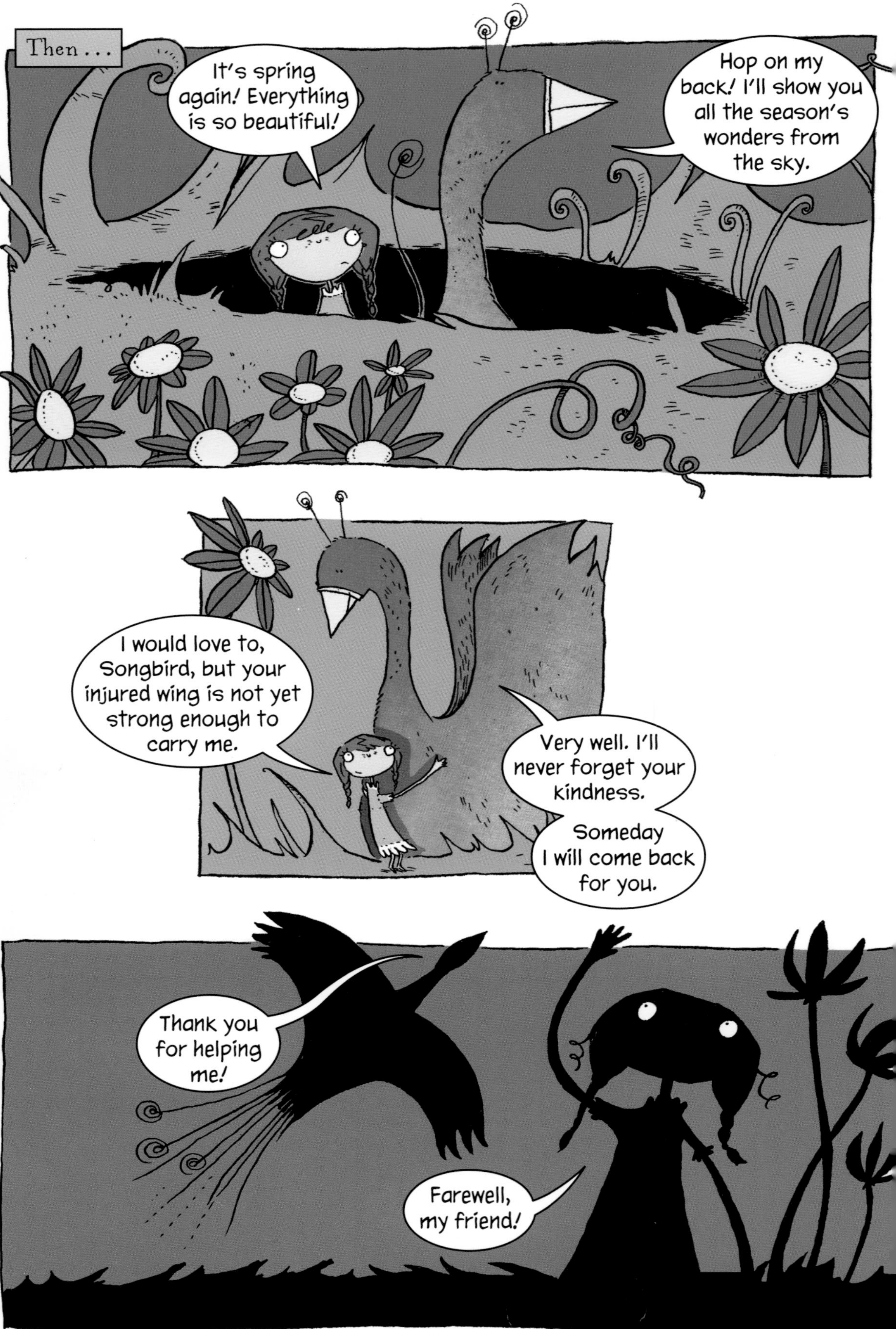
Then . . .
It's spring again! Everything is so beautiful!
Hop on my back! I'll show you all the season's wonders from the sky.
I would love to, Songbird, but your injured wing is not yet strong enough to carry me.
Very well. I'll never forget your kindness.
Someday I will come back for you.
Thank you for helping me!
Farewell, my friend!

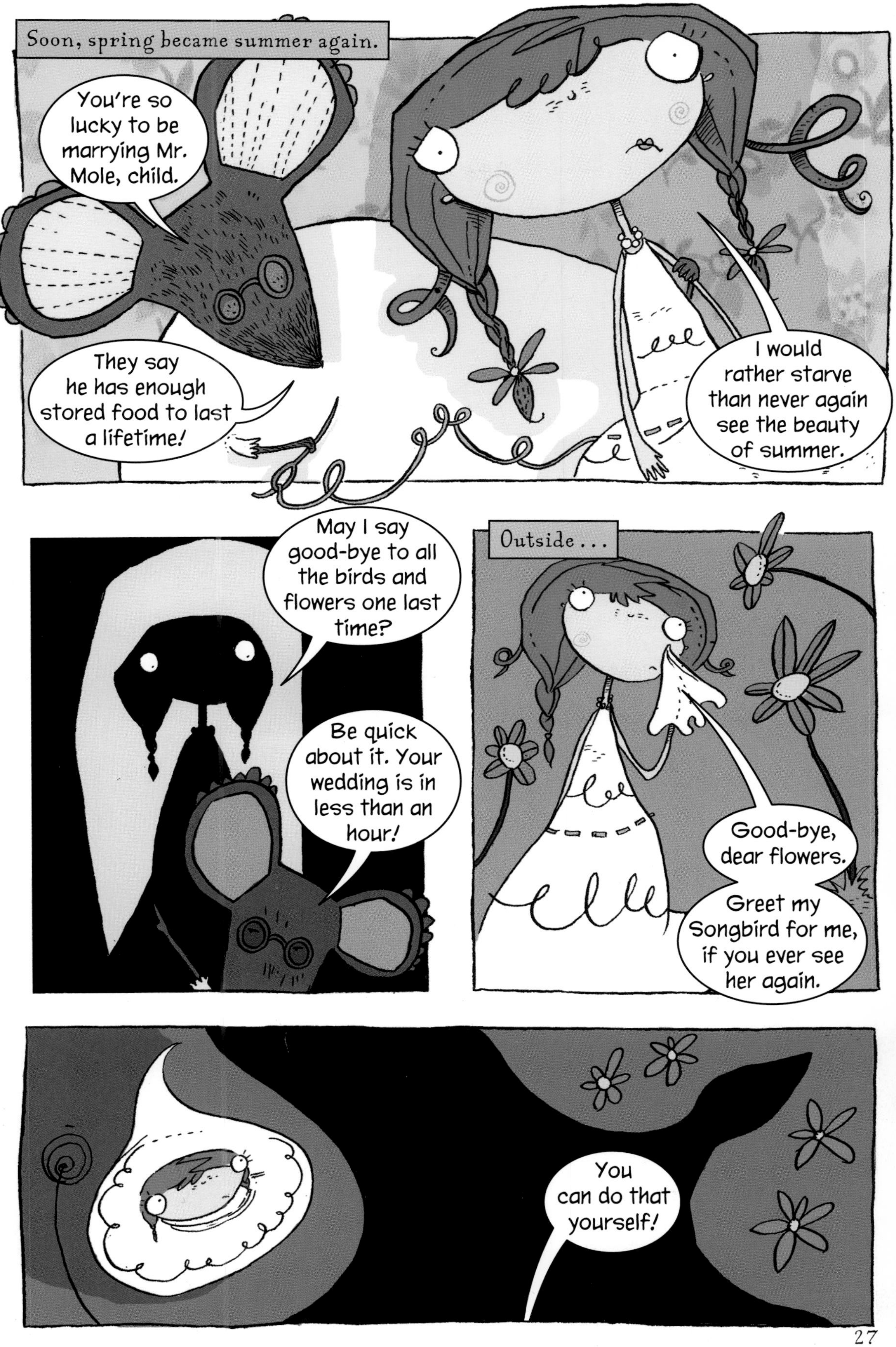

Soon, spring became summer again.
You're so lucky to be marrying Mr. Mole, child.
They say he has enough stored food to last a lifetime!
I would rather starve than never again see the beauty of summer.
May I say good-bye to all the birds and flowers one last time?
Be quick about it. Your wedding is in less than an hour!
Outside . . .
Good-bye, dear flowers.
Greet my Songbird for me, if you ever see her again.
You can do that yourself!

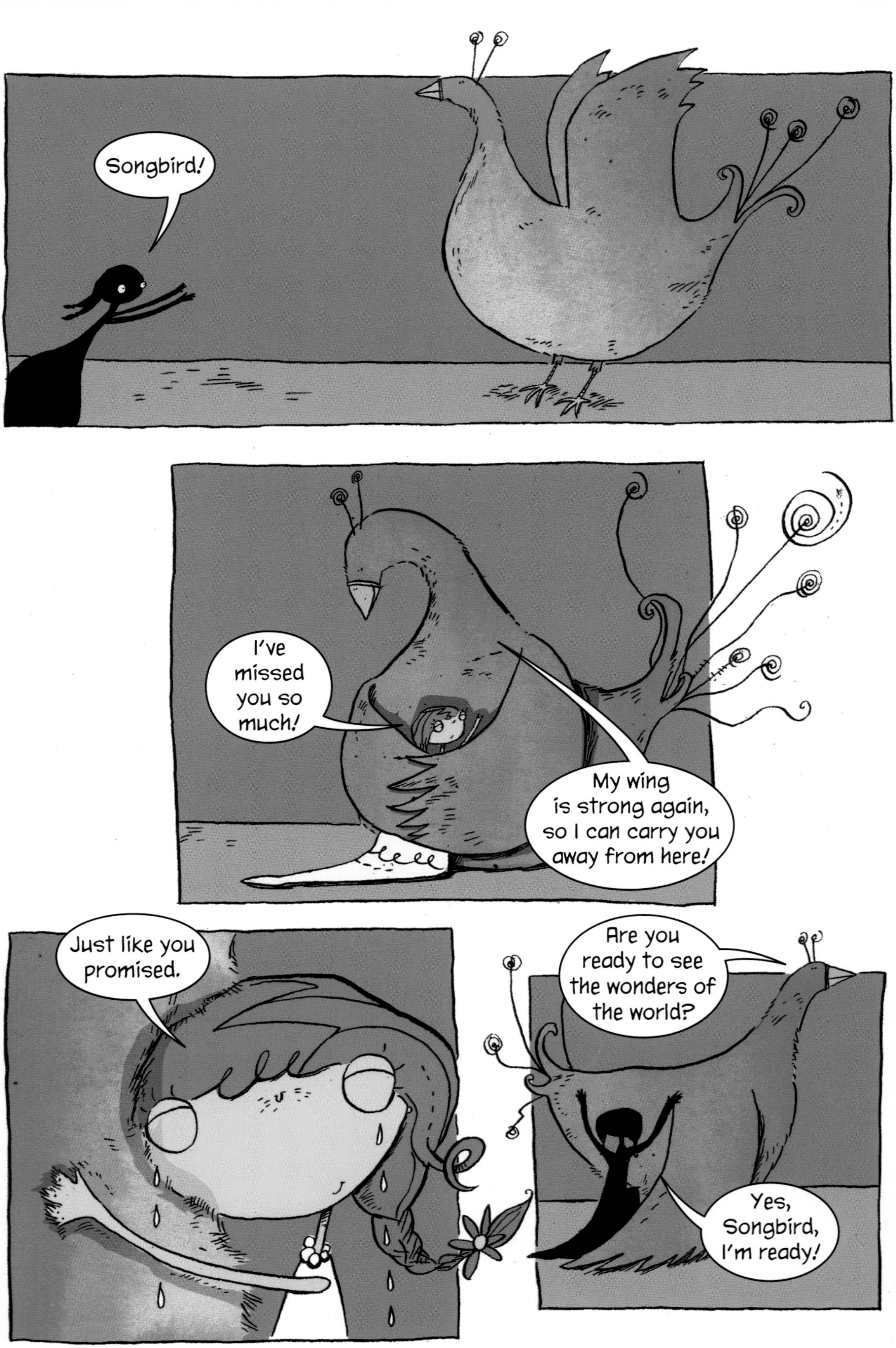
Songbird!
I've missed you so much!
My wing is strong again, so I can carry you away from here!
Just like you promised.
Are you ready to see the wonders of the world?
Yes, Songbird, I'm ready!

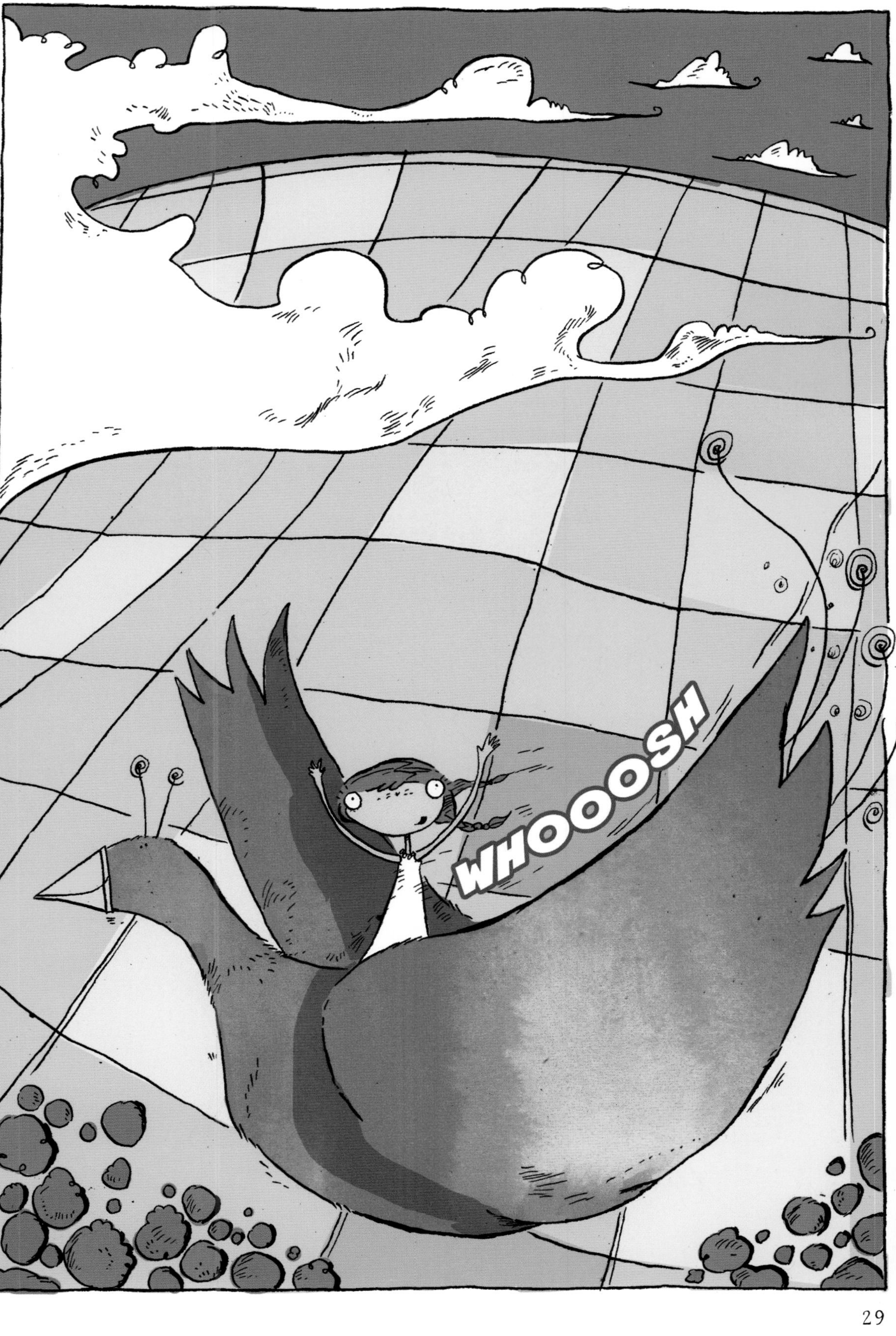
WHOOOOSH

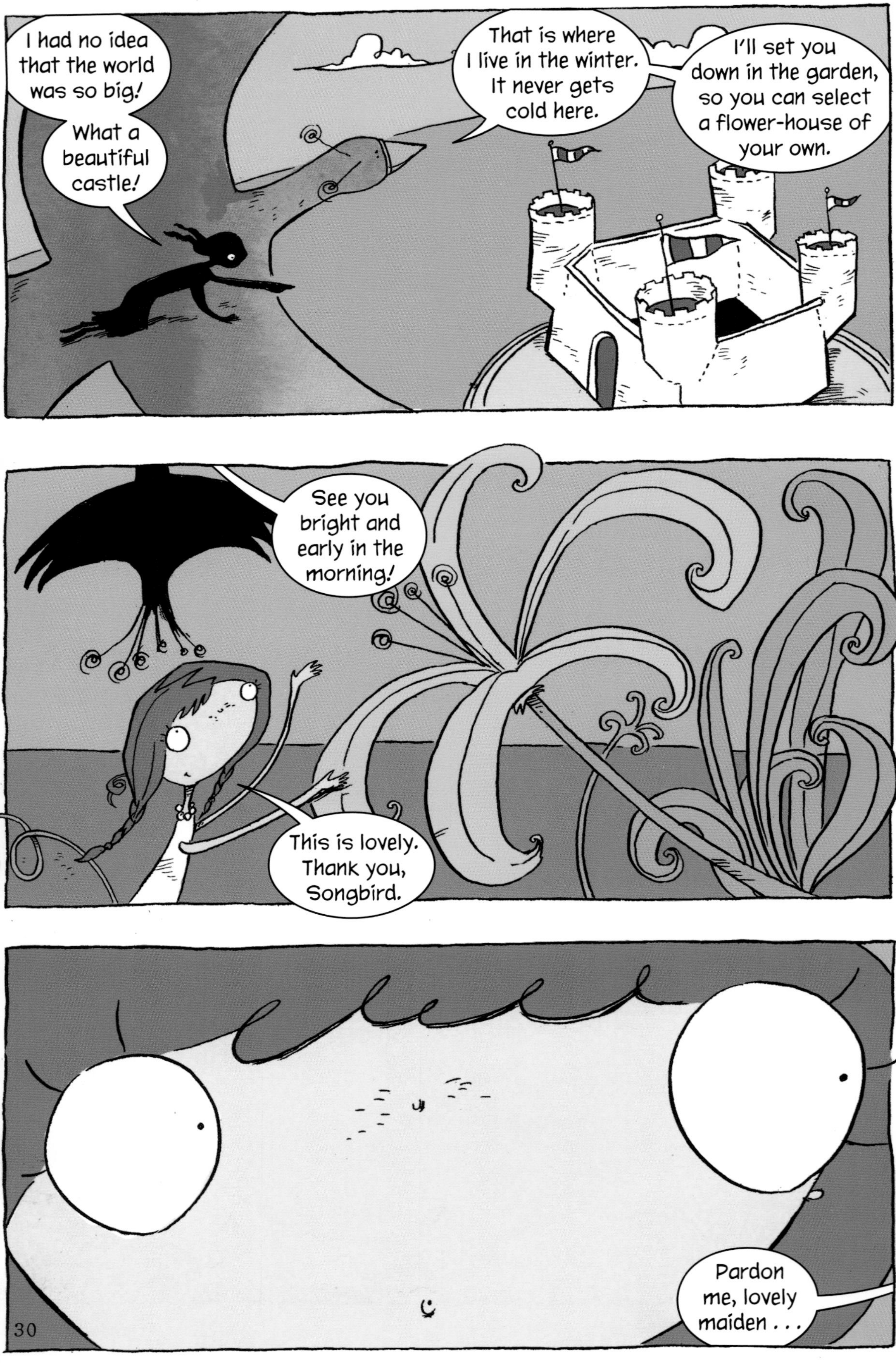
I had no idea that the world was so big!
What a beautiful castle!
That is where I live in the winter. It never gets cold here.
I'll set you down in the garden, so you can select a flower-house of your own.
See you bright and early in the morning!
This is lovely. Thank you, Songbird.
Pardon me, lovely maiden . . .

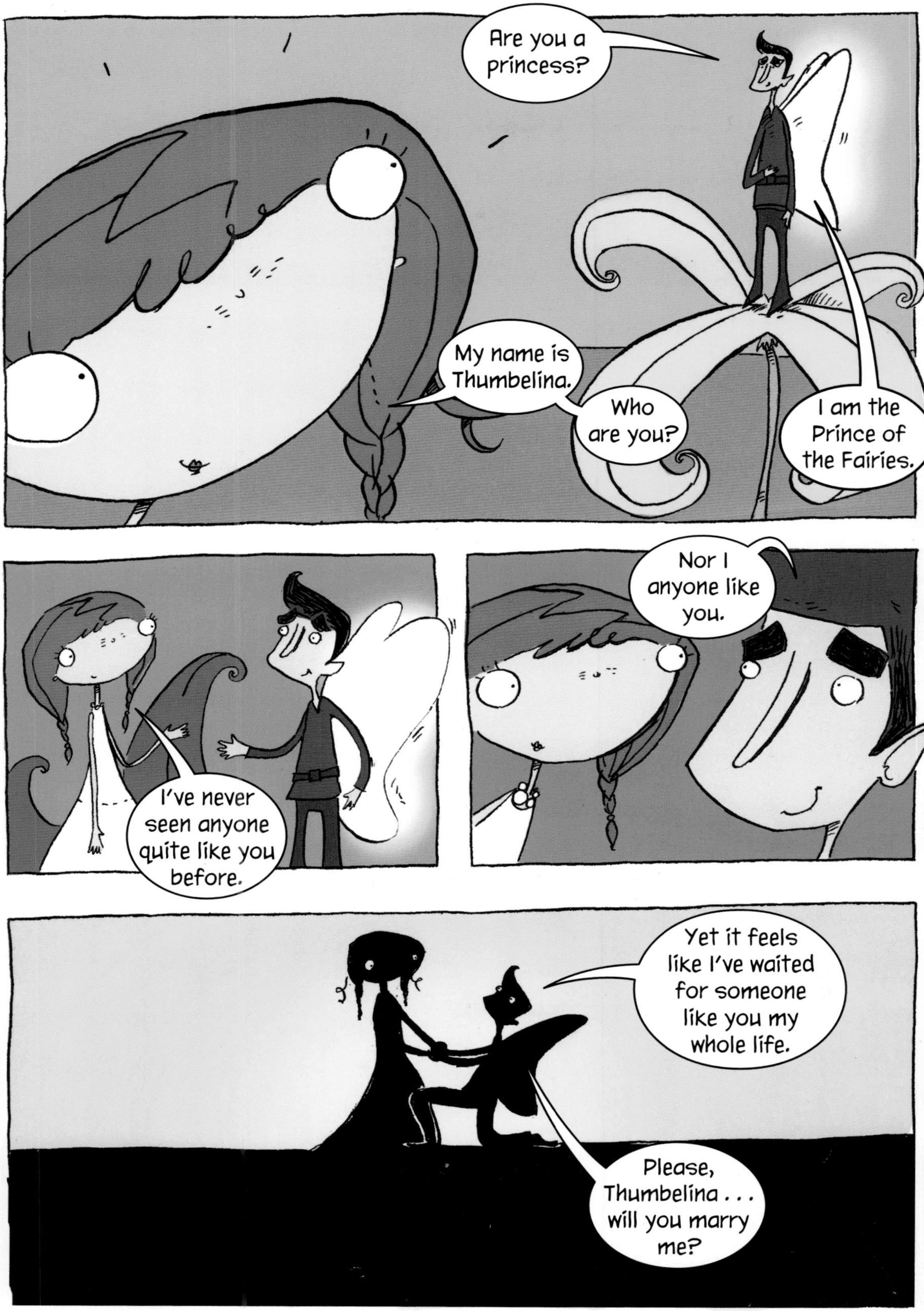
Are you a princess?
My name is Thumbelina.
Who are you?
I am the Prince of the Fairies.
I've never seen anyone quite like you before.
Nor I anyone like you.
Yet it feels like I've waited for someone like you my whole life.
Please, Thumbelina . . . will you marry me?

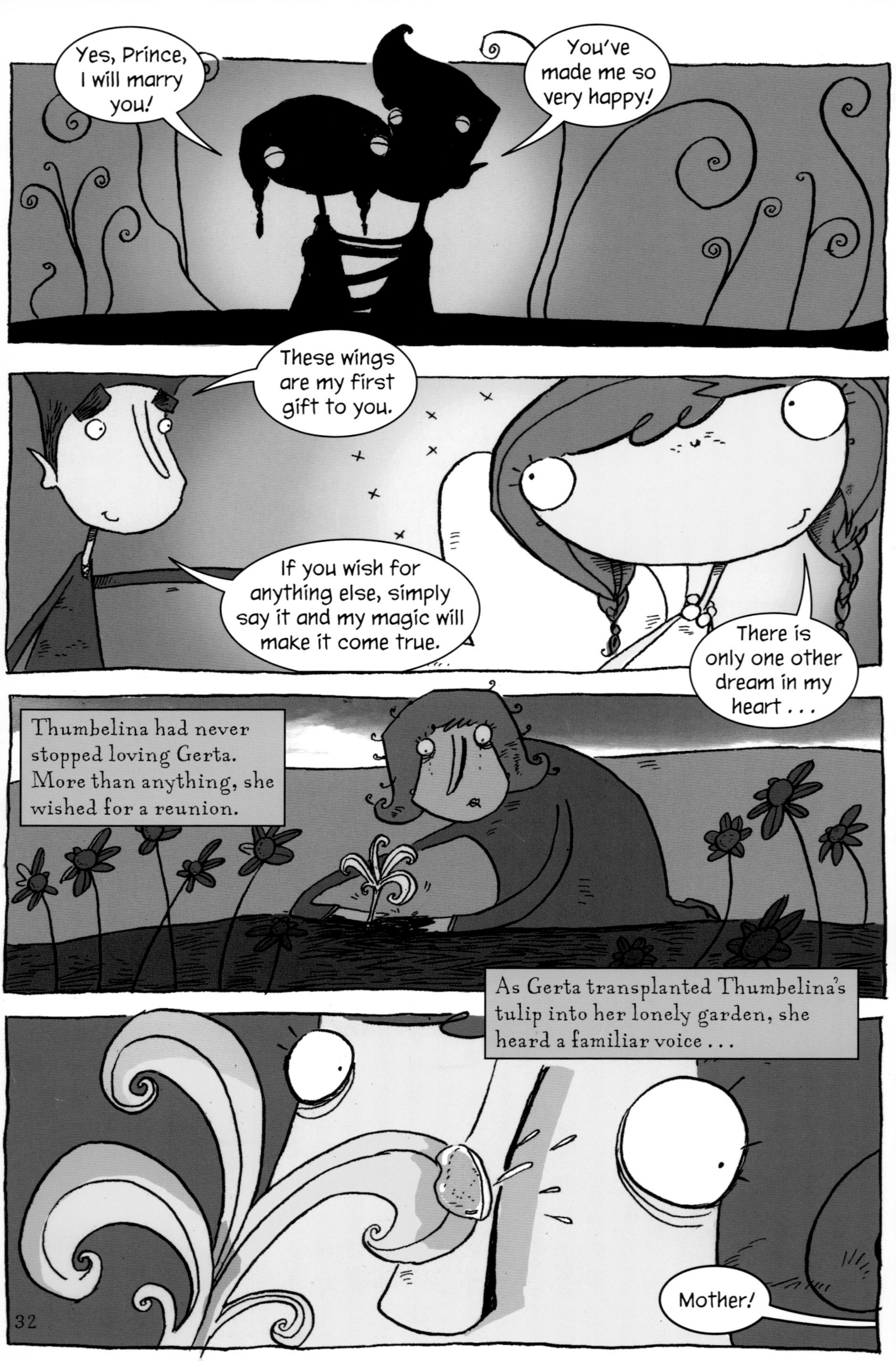

Yes, Prince, I will marry you!
You've made me so very happy!
These wings are my first gift to you.
If you wish for anything else, simply say it and my magic will make it come true.
There is only one other dream in my heart . . .
Thumbelina had never stopped loving Gerta. More than anything, she wished for a reunion.
As Gerta transplanted Thumbelina's tulip into her lonely garden, she heard a familiar voice . . .
Mother!

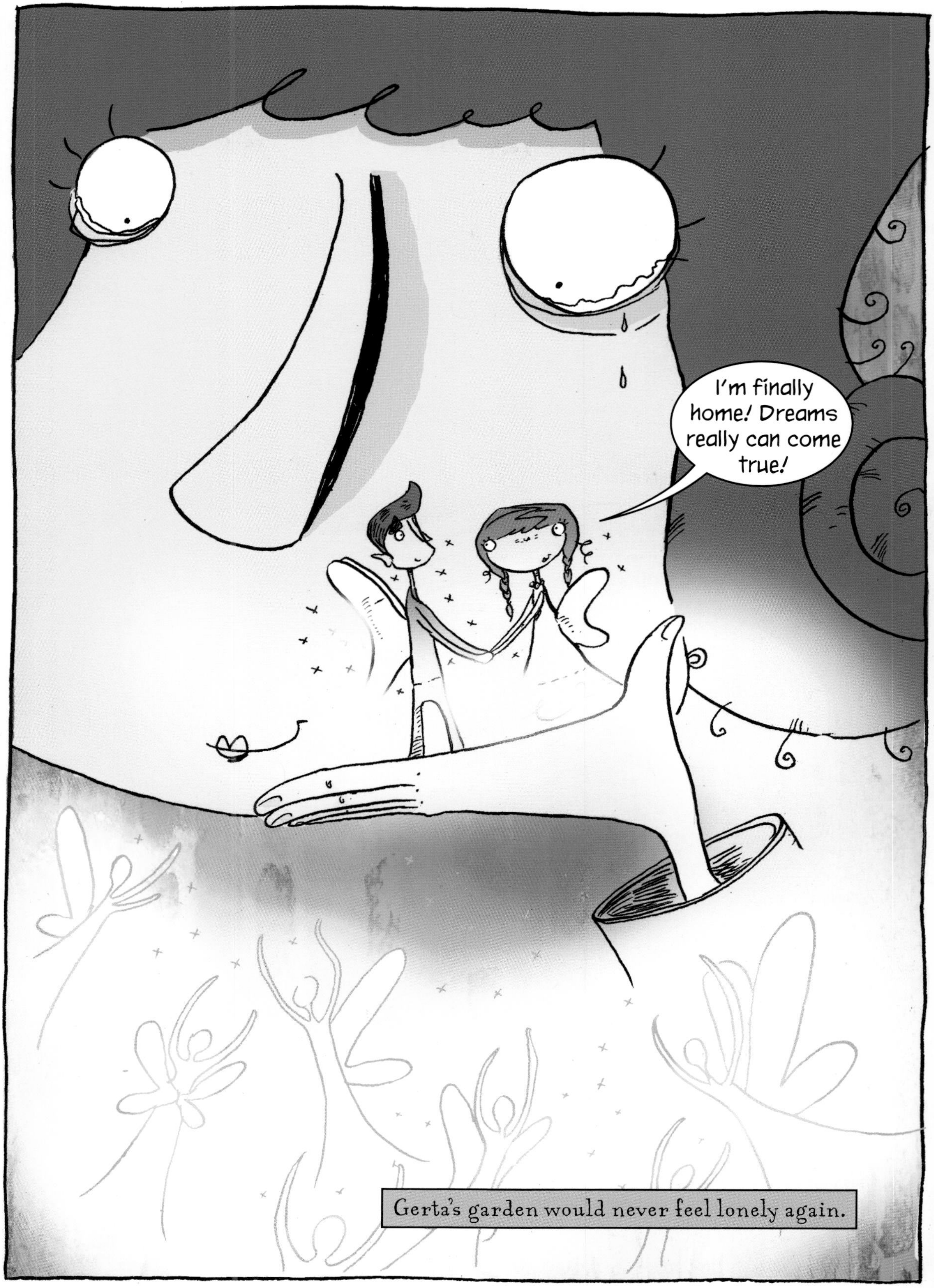
I'm finally home! Dreams really can come true!
Gerta's garden would never feel lonely again.

GLOSSARY

antennas (an-TEN-uhz)—feelers on the heads of insects

burrowing (BUR-oh-ing)—digging a tunnel or hole

fairies (FAIR-eez)—magical creatures with tiny wings

inconvenient (in-kuhn-VEE-nyuhnt)—if something is inconvenient, it causes trouble or difficulty

madam (MAD-uhm)—a formal title for an older woman

maiden (MAYD-uhn)—a formal title for a young, unmarried woman

reunion (ree-YOON-yuhn)—a meeting between people who have not seen each other in a long time

starves (STARVZ)—suffers or dies from lack of food

transplanted (transs-PLANT-id)—moved a plant from one pot to another pot or a garden

THE AUTHOR

HANS CHRISTIAN ANDERSEN

April 2, 1805 – August 4, 1875

Hans Christian Andersen was born in Odense, Denmark. As Hans grew up, he tried many different professions, but none seemed to be a good fit. He eventually found work as an actor and singer, but when his voice changed, he could no longer sing well enough to make a living. Soon after, a friend suggested that he start writing. A short time later, he published his first story, "The Ghost at Palnatoke's Grave."

Andersen's first book of fairy tales was published in 1835. Andersen adored children, so most of his fairy tales focused on them. He continued to write children's stories, publishing one almost every year, until he fell ill in 1872.

Andersen had written more than 150 fairy tales before his death in 1875. His stories have been translated into more than 150 different languages and are still published all over the world. He is considered to be the father of the modern fairy tale.

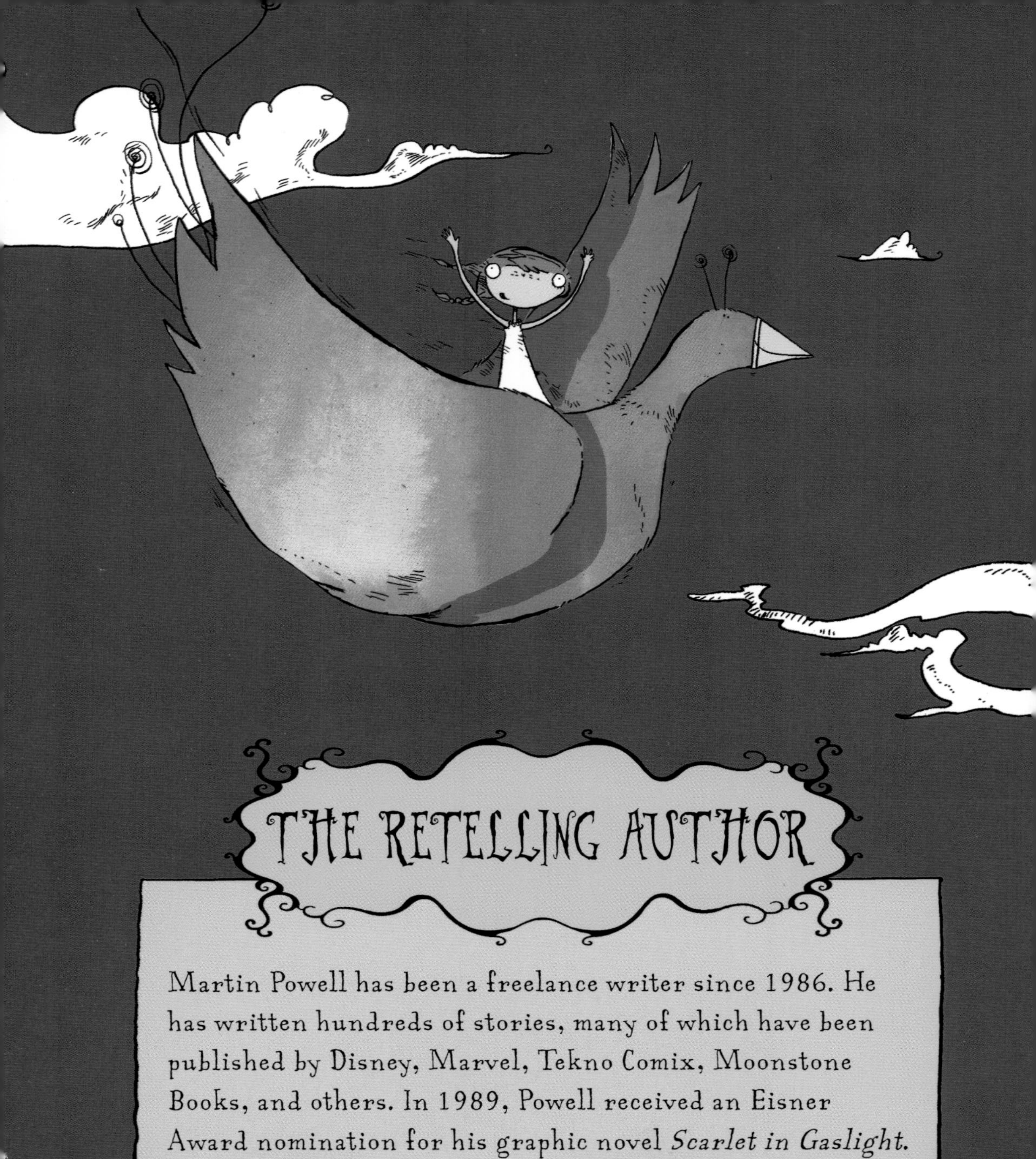

THE RETELLING AUTHOR

Martin Powell has been a freelance writer since 1986. He has written hundreds of stories, many of which have been published by Disney, Marvel, Tekno Comix, Moonstone Books, and others. In 1989, Powell received an Eisner Award nomination for his graphic novel *Scarlet in Gaslight*. This award is one of the highest comic book honors.

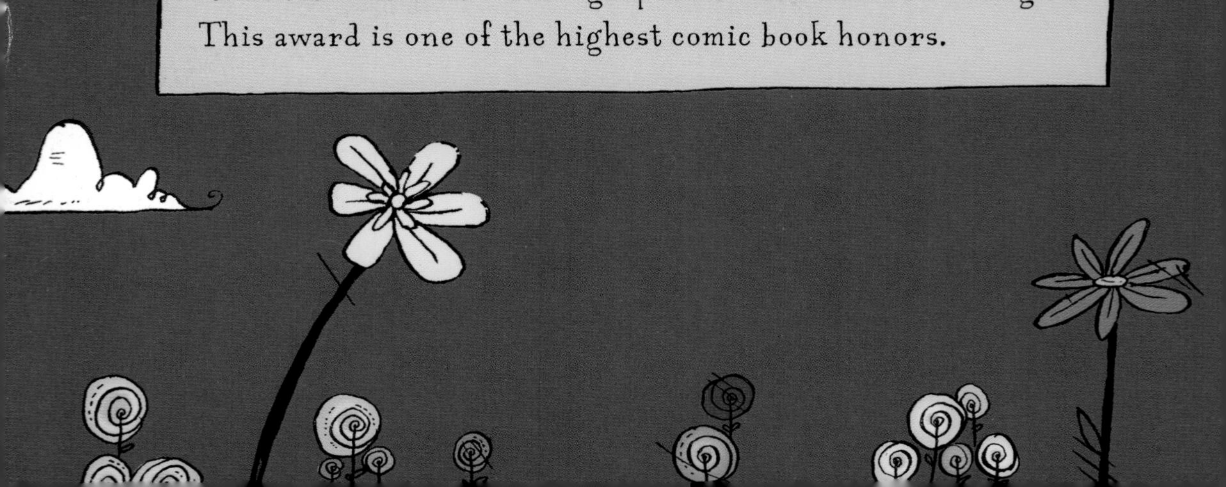

THE ILLUSTRATOR

Sarah Horne was born in Derbyshire, United Kingdom, on a cold November day. Since then, she graduated from Falmouth College of Arts in 2001 and from Kingston University with a master's degree in illustration in 2005. Currently, Sarah lives and works in Wapping, London, and spends many hours sipping tea while working at Happiness At Work Studios.

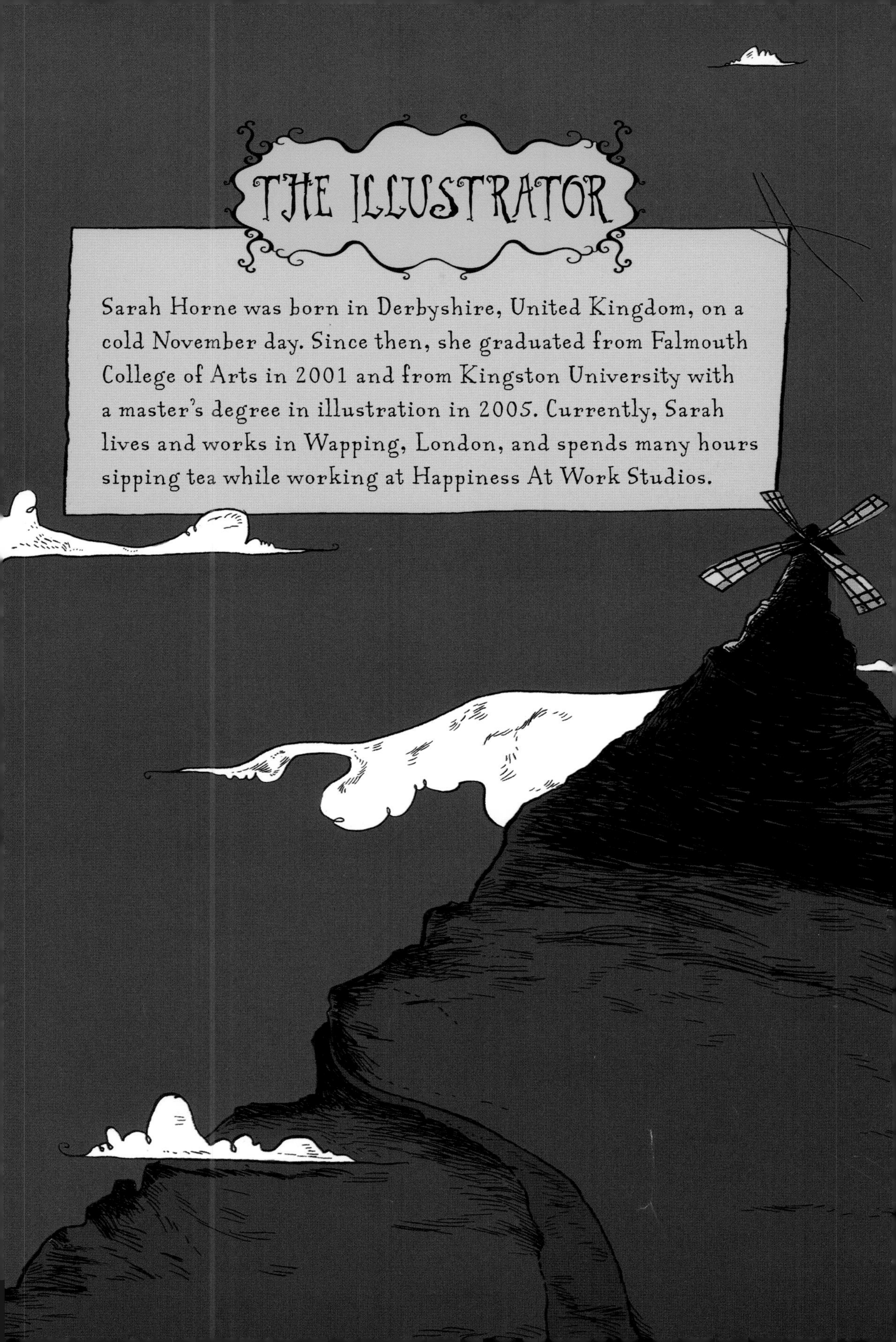

DISCUSSION QUESTIONS

1. Thumbelina struggles to survive in the wild because she's so very small. Do you think life is easier for tall or short people? Explain.

2. Thumbelina and the Fairy Prince fall in love at first sight. Do you believe in love at first sight? Why or why not?

3. Gerta had wanted a child for a very long time before she finally had one of her own. When you grow up, do you think you'll want to have kids? Would you rather have a son or a daughter?

WRITING PROMPTS

1. Miss Mouse wanted Thumbelina to marry Mister Mole even though Thumbelina didn't want to. Have you ever been told to do something that you thought was unfair? What did you do about it?

2. The Fairy Prince makes all of Thumbelina's wishes come true. If you were granted one wish, what would you wish for? Write about how your life would change if your wish was granted.

3. There are many interesting animals in this fairy tale, like the helpful catfish and the old she-toad. Think up your own crazy creature. What kind of animal is it? Can it fly, walk, or swim? What does it like to do? Write about it. Then, draw a picture of your creation.

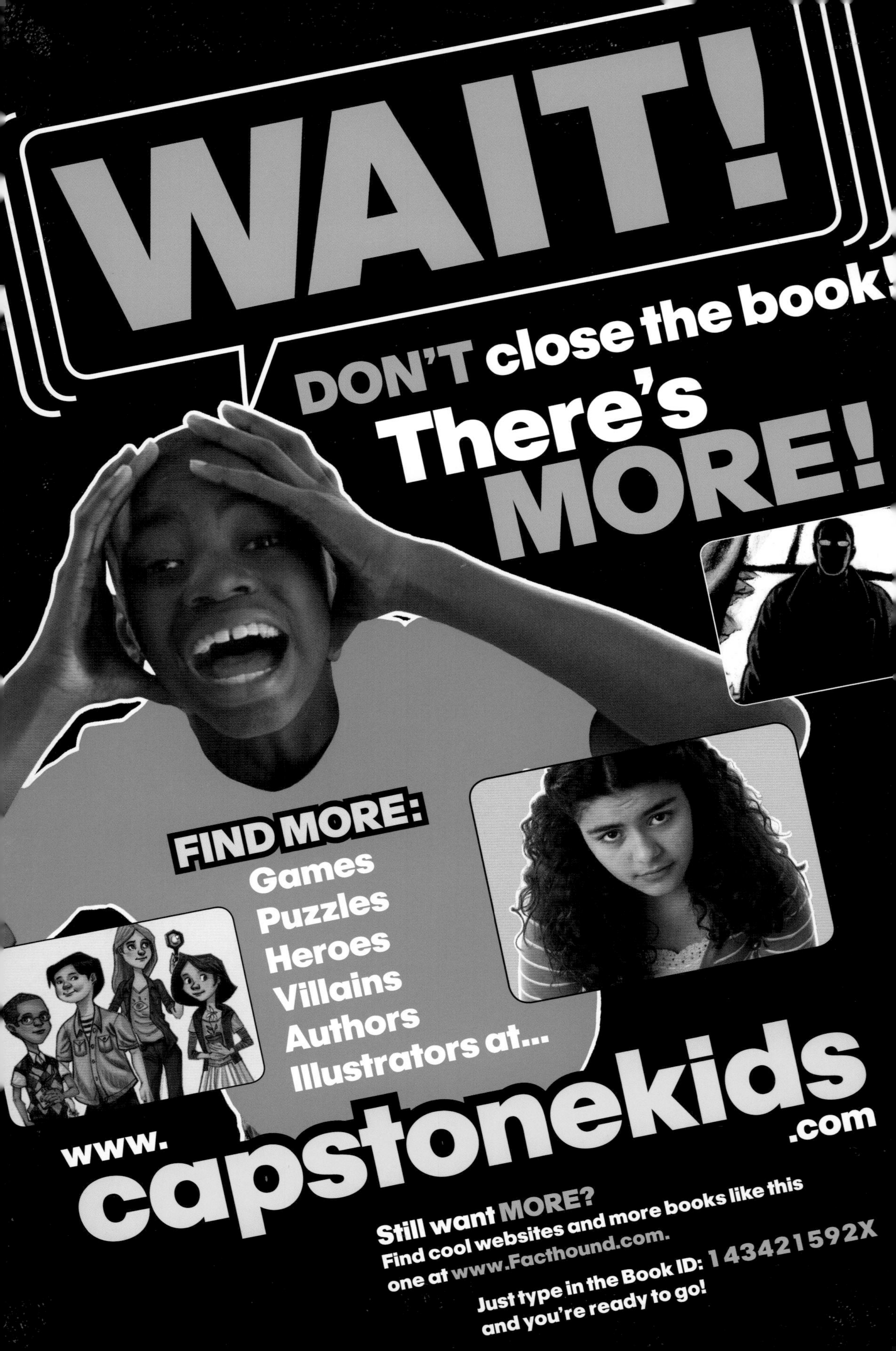
WAIT!
DON'T close the book!
There's MORE!
FIND MORE:
Games
Puzzles
Heroes
Villains
Authors
Illustrators at...
www.
capstonekids
.com
Still want MORE?
Find cool websites and more books like this one at www.Facthound.com.
Just type in the Book ID: 143421592X
and you're ready to go!